Beyond
and
After Life

By

Christine J. Haven

First published by Owl Creek Press

ISBN: 978-0-6152-0420-8

Printed in the United States of America

Dedication

This book is dedicated to all of God's children.

CHAPTERS

Preamble

As David sat, his now oldest living brother, Espie, sat down beside him and said, "I'm going to sit beside the one who is nearer to God," as he smiled at David.

Espie, lived with a superiorly complex, who was always telling everyone about all his inventions that he ever sold. He also claimed he was once a boxer and carried scars that proved he fought in his younger years. Now he was an older thin man in his mid 70s, who wore a brown toupee that didn't fit very well.

David viewed all the people crying in this remodeled living room, a hundred thoughts begin to run through his mind. He realized that this is an old house merely remodeled into a funeral home; folding chairs are aligned in what use to be the living room. The floors were covered with a dark blue carpet and the windows were draped with what some people believe to be "elegant" curtains. Christian prints hung on the walls as this preacher stands near a coffin lined in satin that holds the dearly departed.

David looked around at his siblings, his brother's family and friends that should be celebrating Jim's life instead of mourning his "death" if they only knew of God. It was then that David realized that people do not know that there is no death with God; there is only life.

The Reverend James Dye stood up in front of the mourners, slowly looking from one to another, and he said, "We gather here today to honor the memory of James E. Haven..."

Reverend James Dye was thin, short man in his mid 50s, who wore a dark colored suite, he had dark brown hair and had that wild look in his eyes that made you realize that he was a true Christian.

How sad that this is what this life has come to... Where was this preacher during Jim's life?

1

Did Reverend Dye know of all the trials and tribulations that James went through, not only as an adult, but also as a child?

What consolation did Jim have when he lost his wife to Lupus Disease and was left to raise five of their eight children alone?

Then a very short time after that, Jim lost his oldest child, Kathy, to a massive heart attack. She was only thirty-two years old and left behind four small children. Did he blame God for the departure of his loved ones?

Did Reverend Dye know about the time when Jim was young and lit a match and dropped it into an empty car gasoline tank that exploded and broke his arm, or about the time that in a drunken conversation, Espie told him that no one would build a monument to him?

That statement from Espie' devastated Jim so bad that he tried to commit suicide. David never forgot that conversation even though he was quite young and sober at the time. It was just a few short months ago that he came back to visit his ailing brother and David reminded Jim of that particular conversation. David let him know that there is a monument built to him and that monument was his children. Through his children, he will live forever. That made him smile and he nodded his acknowledgment of understanding to David.

Did Reverend Dye ever really talk to Jim about life?

Did he, the preacher, not know that life would someday leave all of us?

Did he ever talk with Jim about what to expect after life?

Why did the preacher, not teach his flock that life is just part of God's Promise to each of us?

As Reverend Dye continued speaking, they sat and listened to the him, David's brother, Espie, cried for their deceased brother, Jim.

David knew in his heart that when he started out on his twenty-five hundred mile journey to Wooster, Ohio, why he had to be there. It was not to say good-bye to his brother. It was to try and help his family and friends understand that Jim will live forever as long as they never forget his touch and that he has taken a journey that someday we will all take.

David always thought that preachers were there to help people through the endurances of life – to help them understand what life is about and to help people in their time of need. Most people look to religion to understand life and death. But do the preachers not know about life and death?

Is it possible that they, the preachers, do not have a clear understanding of this matter?

Where is their guidance when their congregation needs them?

In our book, ***Holy Graduel***, David's story tells of how he came to God, and how He is continually in all of our lives. ***Conveyance of Eternal Love***, is our book that explains of confusion in people about Him, the Creator, and also, it tells of His Love that is with all of us.

After releasing our first two Books and talking to many people around the country, we soon realized that people do not understand what life and death are about. Our first books touched on the subject of life and death but even we did not go into detail. Hopefully, this Book, ***Byond and After Life***, answers most of the questions that we all have had about life. This book goes directly into details of where we came from, why we are here and what happens after this life ends. The answers are abound us.

David recalled that when he became a minister, he was taught how to counsel couples before he would officiate over their weddings, but he never instructed people how to teach their children about life. He was taught about how Christians are saved, but never learned what true afterlife was. He was told that God created Adam and Eve and that was where we all came from, but never learned much about creation that is not mentioned in our Bibles. The real problem is the clergy, and those who proclaim to be ministers, never knew or were never taught the answers to these problems. But the problem is not one from just religions, it also comes from our parents who were never taught or knew the truth.

During the fall of 1996, when God's Angels entered into David's and my life, we learned the answers of before and after life, but we didn't realize that most people didn't know the answers to these questions – their questions, the same questions that we also once had.

It was then that we knew, with God's Angels' help we would write this book that would help others as they face the most important questions of their lives and death.

Creation

We must try to think outside of the box of life. Because all that we know and understand comes from this life that we live, for that is what we learn and understand and this life we live is reality to us.

The latest theory of the big bang of the Universe is that everything started smaller than the point of a needle, and we do not know if this was the first big bang or not.

As told to David from God's Angels, we are presently in the fifth cycle of life. Other cycles may be occurring at the same time or there could be many more before or after this cycle, and where every cycle may have its individual and different reality.

During the last part of 2007, some astronomers believed that they have discovered a solar system much like the Milky Way, but rotating the opposite direction than our Milky Way. The Milky Way rotates clockwise; this newly found solar system rotates counter-clockwise. The astronomers believe that this newly found solar system may have been formed from another or second big bang. To understand the gravity field in the Universe, we must look at our world; we have a northern and southern hemisphere that rotates in different directions when viewed from its center at the equator. This rotation is demonstrated by the direction that water flows in the northern and southern hemispheres.

(In the northern hemisphere water flows clockwise, and in the southern hemisphere water flows counter clockwise.)

In both hemispheres water flows to the equator, from the east to the west, and that is the same direction that we see the Sun rising and setting. Does this mean that the two solar systems directions were created from and following different gravity fields?

We don't know yet, allow the astronomy scholars to find the answer because it is not our concern.

Albert Einstein's Theory was correct about as matter moves faster, matter becomes smaller. As we move out from the center of the big bang, we move faster and faster, and as we travel faster everything becomes smaller and that includes the distances between the matter.

As we travel, to us it looks like the distances become larger, but everything is getting smaller as we, the matter, closes back into itself.

At the end of this cycle, we will close back to the size of a needle's point once again, and everything will be correct for God – the Creator, then we will begin another cycle – another big bang, if needed.

When we look at space in the Universe, we must think of distances in light years. For instance, if you were to stand at one end of the Universe and have a friend stand at the other end of the Universe and if you had a very bright light and shone it towards your friend, it would take twelve billion years for that light to reach your friend. That is an awesome span of space. The miles, feet and inches that we measure here on earth are nothing compared to light years.

Therefore, all on earth places us as the center of our individual Universes, and that makes a mere human's life here on earth as grandeur in God's eyes. But all that exist is reality and including the Universe is a concept of God's. Time is not part of God's Reality. But time is needed for our lives and that, too, is part of God's Master Plan.

Time exists in this reality. In God's Reality, He or His Angels can move forward or backwards in time. All that exist including time is for living things. Everything in this Universe was designed for all living things. Because time was needed and created for all living things by God

And if we look at the Universe, we will see there is matter and space – nothing. The space that is nothing is God's thoughts without humans or any other living matter within it.

God is the Supreme Creator of everything. We have listened to many descriptions of what people believe God is and what He looks like. The most popular one is that He looks like an old man with white hair and a white beard; a very prestigious looking man. However, recently we had a friend tell us that he thought God is more of a form of energy and the only word he could think of to describe Him was that He was like an Entity. Our friend did not think that He was a male or female, but more or less like an aura with a very bright light. Living in this reality, we will never be able to see or understand His Creation until we arrive into His Reality, after life. Do we need to understand everything about God to know He does exist?

If we decide to study or travel to distant stars and planets, we may find some of the secrets held beyond our intelligence, if we do not then it is not our concern. For each of us are at the correct place in time that was meant for us to be.

Someday, all will be gone; the stars and planets and everything that is now on and in those planets will be gone; the beautiful automobiles that we drive, the wonderful homes that we live in and the great lands that we admire will all be gone. No matter will last because there is an end to everything. And everything will be recycled back in to God's Creation.

Can you imagine everything that we think of and know came from God's thoughts?

To understand Creation of this Universe, think of yourself as being as small as an ant and you are standing in a rain forest like place with tall green things reaching high above you toward the sky. You watch as another ant carries a large diametric red rope about twice as long as its body. This ant struggles and pulls this large rope along through this jungle setting. You know, for you can feel in your heart that this little guy is very proud of his find and is taking it back to friends in their tunnels that they call home.

Slowly you drift up higher and higher as you try to keep your eyes focused on the little ant. Soon he disappears below as it now becomes apparent that you were in a grassy patch of someone's front yard.

All at once you are standing beside a young teenage girl on a street corner in New York City, as people and cars hurry by. You know for you can feel deep in your heart that this young girl is a run-a-way from her family in West Virginia. You can feel her hurt and pains of what her mother and father gave her when they repeatedly told her she was no good and stupid and abused her.

Slowly you drift up higher and higher until you cannot see the girl but only the large city laid out below you.

Next you view a large city in the mid-west, in which you are now standing in the back of a church. Soon a preacher walks upon the stage. He gives his sermon that includes, "those who do not believe

Jesus died for them on the cross are lost" and how "God only loves the ones who come to, belong to and believe in this church for those are only the true saved ones upon Earth."

Slowly you drift up through the church's roof as you float higher and higher. Within a few minutes you cannot see the church but only the North American Continent. As you travel farther into space, you now see the world below as its beautiful colors become apparent to you, but still you travel farther into space, now you look around yourself and see the universe that surrounds you. You view the Earth as only a little white speck of light in the darkness of space as you also see many other planets and stars in the same manner.

You are seeing all that God owns.

The little ant that you saw carrying the red string belongs to God.

The young teenager who thinks no one cares about her belongs to God.

The preacher in the church belongs to God.

God owns everything, yet He allows every living thing to make its own individual choices in its life. God allowed the ant to be proud of the string that he found. God allowed the teenage girl to feel down because she thinks no one loves her. God allowed the preacher to lie to his congregation about the only direction to Him is by believing Jesus died for you on the cross and about those who are or are not saved. God created all of this, does all of this and gave us everything else we have because He Loves us.

Look at all that is happening in the world today.

On a Sunday in Florida, Dale Earnhardt died in a stock car race. Many people cried and placed offerings at his place of business.

In recent days there have been earthquakes in India and Central America that killed thousands, how many sent offerings and cried for those people?

People were killed in terrorist attacks in Europe the other day, how many sent offerings and cried for those people?

Yet it was reported that Dale Earnhardt died because he was not wearing a neck brace/ helmet that was designed to save the life of a race car driver in crashes like the one that took his life and they were approved by the Racing Board. The people in India, Central America and Europe that died were just trying to live their lives in today's world.

Who should we cry for?

Do you really care about others?

We comprehend in the only way we can - the human way of thinking. Therefore, we believe God must think as we do because we are intelligent and we cannot be wrong. Yet, we do not care about the struggles or happiness of others, God cares about these things.

People of today think of God as an outsider, one who does not know or care about us. But we are not without God; He dwells within everything here on earth as well as all that is in the Heavens. But people's self-centered ideas and thoughts place God not with or within us but instead outside of themselves.

God loves us. He gave Himself - His Creation to us; Love is giving yourself to another. Love is allowing another who you have given yourself to, to make their individual choices in life. Choices are also individual thoughts, ideas and concepts.

Thoughts, ideas and concepts that place domination over others are self-centered ideas and these remove God from within oneself. When this occurs, in God's eyes that individual is No-thing, for he is oblivious to God.

Look not through your eyes with your thoughts, ideas and concepts, but instead look with feeling from your heart at all things around you, then you shall see as God sees.

Break open a piece of wood and God is there. Over turn a rock and God is there.

Everything…things like science, theology, chemistry, mathematics and physics came from God… Everything that we think and do came from God. Even the concept of Evil came from Him, human created the actions of Evil, but all that man created was known by God.

You must pardon us because David's memory grows dim as his body grows old and weak, but his memory of God remains strong. And as he recalls in mathematics, it was said that there is an equation for everything and when the equation is found for life it will be a one digit equation. The equation for life is zero because no matter how many zeros you add to it or remove from it the answer is always zero. And the zero is the only number, an equation, that goes back into itself because it is a continuous line, the only number that begins with itself and ends with itself – God. For God is the beginning and the ending to everything.

The only need for living was for us to experience what our actions will bring. Experiencing reactions of our actions. A place where each experiences and learns from the experiences of others through the endurance of life.

When we die and go back to the dirt from which we came from is not our concern, and the dirt that we will lay in until the end of this time is not our concern. As it is not our concern when this cycle began or when it is time for it to end. And it does not matter who owns what we leave behind.

This cycle may go far beyond when our lives end just as it was here long before our lives began. It is not our concern what happens after our demise! Our concern is what we do in this time that we were allowed to live within because we do not know everything. We have taken the first steps from when our ancestors, the first one-cell animal, walked upon the earth, and we will learn until the end of time.

Nothing is real in our reality, everything was created by and for the Creator; we came from nothing and we will return to nothing. The only thing that will remain is the Energy that lives within each individual. All of the matter that made us will be re-cycled into the Universe. The Energy of our known life will continue, and that Energy is the individual's life experiences that will live forever with the Creator.

Neil deGrasse Tyson
Astrophysicist American Museum of Natural History

Recognize that the very molecules that make up your body, the atoms that construct the molecules are traceable to the crucibles that were once the center of high mass stars that exploded their chemically enriched guts into the galaxy enriching pristine gas clouds with the chemistry of life, so that we are connected; to each other biologically, to the earth chemically and to the rest of the Universe atomically. That's kind of cool. That makes me smile. And I actually feel quite large at the end of that. It's not that we are better than the Universe; we are part of the Universe. We are in the Universe and the Universe is in us.

The DNA is Born

The Creation of God's Universe also contains the DNA that flows through our bodies. And that DNA contains a "Clock" that knows how long the body will last as natural without assistance or help from others. Someday, we may be able to control our bodies where we may grow new hands or feet or repair disabilities, the limits of humans are presently unknown. And someday, people will be able to read the last days of life from the deceased DNA.

(Who and what killed that person because the DNA is the recorded actions of the body)

To understand DNA (Deoxyribonucleic acid), one must go back to understanding the basics of reconstructing the building blocks of life.

Reconstructing DNA does not mean replacing damaged or destroyed DNA. Reconstructing DNA refers to laying the plan of building blocks of DNA in offspring, a living thing the same as you are.

The DNA is the pattern of how every part of the body is laid out and how each inner part reacts with each part of the body. The human body nor any other design could be replicated without the design and that is the DNA of recorded life. And the DNA contains the reasons for change that come from the endurances of existing life.

In procreation, one is placing the same design that is contained within that person into their offspring; all that the parents did (endured) is contained (recorded) within the parents DNA and is placed into its offspring.

If the DNA is not transferred to its offspring then the offspring would not look or act like the parents did, then the offspring would look like and act differently as another unknown and different animal. Whereas, the DNA is the total recorded experiences of the parents passed into their child, and the parents contained all the recorded experiences of their ancestors that is passed on to their offspring.

Once the first one-cell animal was created and moved upon the earth, it carried what today we call our DNA. This DNA is linked back to the first living plant on earth.

We do not know what scientist may find in the future. The limits of scientists are left up to those individuals. But for sure, your DNA goes back to the first one-cell animal on earth.

(What is known by and recorded in our DNA is not a curse that continues seven generations as claimed in the Christian Bible.)

To help understand DNA, we must re-view some of the stories in the Bible. The Torah and Old Testament of the Christian Bible does not say where Adam's and Eve's sons found their wives. But if their son's wives came from other tribes, then Adam's and Eve's grandchildren were not the true chosen children of God, but if Adam and Eve had daughters too, and if their grandchildren came from only Adam's and Eve's children, did those children come from incestuous. But the act of incest is written into the Torah as being forbidden by God, but if the people in the Jewish Religion do not accept Adam's and Eve's sons' wives as their daugthers, what different tribe did they come?

If they came from different tribles, are they true born Jews?

If that is so, where did the grandchildren of Adam and Eve come from?

The Torah states, the decents of Adam and Eve are the only true children of God.

Were their grandchilden truly born Jews?

Once David asked the Angel Joleen, "How did Lock's daughters procreate with Lock?

"Was their offspring not retarded and disabled or deformed as incested children are today?"

She answered, "They, their DNA, were stronger than it is today."

Today, we can find frogs and toads living in the hot deserts. In the dry seasons, they are underground and when it rains they come out and live upon the earth, and then they procreate as needed. A few species can change their sex and other species can procreate without a mate, humans do not or do that today.

The natural odors of our bodies helped our ancient ancestors' select a mate that would strengthen their DNA. Everything was natural. There were no deodorants or colognes or perfumes to cover the natural fragrance that God gave us. Today, we cover our bodies with smells to hide our weaknesses. Sure we need to make ourselves smell better, but we lost our natural instinct on picking out our mate. Hence, we need to find better ways in selecting a mate today.

Our DNA, is the things recorded on our DNA that goes back to the beginning of the lives of our ancestry which began when that first one-cell animal lived on earth.

I am sorry if the thought that your ancestors were once a worm or lower than that, makes you sick. But if your ancestors did not live long enough to procreate, then you would not be here. Whatever your ancestors had to do to live was the way of life that was meant to be back then. We need not act as the one-cell animal lived, times have changed. The way our ancestors acted toward each other has changed with time; many more people live today and live closer together than before.

When David was young, he thought that each girl would grow up looking like her mother, and if her mother was fat, he knew that this girl would someday look just like her mother, fat. And if he liked the girl, it did not matter what her mother looked like because he would be marrying the girl and not her mother.

Now, he knows that this girl will someday be the same as her parents. And that girl, will look and act as her family did. And in the same context, she, the daughter, may act the same as her friends of today. Because if she accepts her friends of today, someday she may be the same as they.

(If a woman today has an evil family member or a homosexual friend, she may be evil or homosexual someday. Because she has already said what her family and friends did or their actions are okay, acceptable for her. It is a little step for her to walk in their shoes.)

Once the male places his sperm within the female, his DNA does not add any more to the DNA of his offspring, but her (the mother's) DNA will continue to add to the unborn child until its birth. And then her DNA will not add any more to the newly born child's DNA. From the point of birth on, the parents are no more than peers to their child. But usually the parents will continue to influence the child until that child leaves home. From this young age and unto death, peers influence the human and its actions are engraved upon its DNA that will be added to and placed upon its DNA. Then his offspring will also carry that which was added to it. This phenomenon continues from generation to generation.

Many times the father or mother will change their direction in life after procreation of a child, and will not understand why the child does not act or think as they do.

How did the father act before procreation?

Is it any different than the way the child now acts?

Also, it may be because the child's DNA did not come just from the father alone, it came from the DNA (recorded experiences) of all his ancestors back to when that first one-cell animal crawled upon the earth. And the mother's DNA also contains her ancestors DNA. What did she and her ancestors endure?

All of that is also placed upon the child. The child does not need to follow what his parents claimed fit their needs alone because the child's ancestors may have had different feelings about life. So did the concepts come only from its parents?

His feelings may have come from other DNA records that were placed upon the parents DNA.

Maybe the style of the child is the same way that his ancestors acted. His actions today may not have been dominant as on his father's DNA. Also let's add, the father's DNA is only half of the child's DNA because the mother was another first part of the child's DNA.

Can we expect our children to be religious as we became in our years?

NO!

David has counseled many parents who do not understand why their children are so different.

Many times he has been told things like, "We raised our children the same. They have the same father and mother, but they are as different as night and day. How can that be?

Where did we go wrong?"

At this point David takes them through a step-by-step scenario of how the DNA works. First, we need to look at where the father was in his life at the time of conception. i.e.: was he drinking or doing drugs?

Did he have a relationship with God?

Then the same thing with the mother. Then we need to look at the family tree. What were the ancestors like?

Now let's move on to the child. Where are his influences? What are his friends like?

Is the child a strong personality?

Was he a follower of a leader?

You see, you cannot take a ball of string and pull out just one strand and see the picture. You have to look at everything.

The father's DNA did not add to the child after procreation, and remember that the mother's DNA did not add to her child's DNA after the child was born. Thus, the parents did not add to the child's DNA after birth.

Our personal demands should not be placed upon others just as we should not place our demands of things that we have learned throughout our lives after our children were born upon our children or other people, friends that we met throughout our lives.

When two people marry, they become as one, and when they have a child, the one then becomes two - two people with different desires and perhaps different concepts.

The DNA should have more influence on the natural functions than the human concepts, but the DNA does contain all concepts that our ancestors thought, felt and did, as well as friends.

During the early 2000s, David had an aunt, that he really didn't know very well, who was dying. This aunt lived in Kentucky and for some unknown reason, he drove back there from California to see her.

David never knew his father had a sister that he was so close to before. David's aunt told him that his dad had written a poem for her that she recited in grade school and won first place with. David could not recall all of it but it started something like this, "God made man and man made dirt." He never knew his dad was religious until she told him that.

It was at that time that David met his cousin, Jack, for the first time. Since David's mother did not like his dad's side of the family they were not close to any of his aunts or uncles growing up. David was astonished seeing Jack for the first time, they looked alike; they looked so much alike that they could have been twins, only Jack was 6 years older than David.

From that point on, they have talked many times. David found both have much in common; they both have owned Royal Enfield Motorcycles, they both were owners and like Honda 750cc Motorcycles, and they both have ridden across the country, and they both like the southwestern part of the country. They both wore beards but David's was shorter than Jack's, and they both have light blue eyes. Also they both worked as mechanics, Jack was once an auto mechanic and David was a heavy truck and forklift mechanic. They both like airplanes, presently Jack is building an ultra light plane from scratch, while David has been thinking about building and flying a power paraglider. Both of them are very intelligent, and they both have been divorced and both are now married to younger women.

One day while David was at Jack's home, Jack's son, who had never met David, rode up on his motorcycle, and he said, "Boy, you guys look like twins."

Yes, all of our characteristics are engraved on our DNA.

Scholars have stated that someday when a person leaves his DNA at a crime scene it will be like leaving his Driver's License because DNA contains everything including what a person looks like, where he lives and where he works.

The DNA carries everything that we and our ancestors did in life. Our Souls contain the same as our DNA and that will be engraved upon the Angel-within, and that Angel in congregation with other Angels is God. And that, our memories of life, will live with God forever. Because as individuals we are the littlest part of the smallest point of a needle of God's Creation.

All is recorded into our DNA, everything that we have ever done. And someday, we will be able to read all that you have done. In other words, if you commit a crime, the law will be able to read from your memory how you were involved in that crime. The lawless will have no place to hide.

After the first one-cell thing that carried God's Master plan in its DNA moved about upon the world, evolution brought all plant and animal life forth which grew into life. It was during those years that followed, early man multiplied and began to spread out in parts of the earth. The DNA was strong in those early years of reproduction. Brothers and sisters could procreate and produce healthy, strong offspring. As time went on and the population grew, the DNA became weaker. This is attributed to the inner breeding.

Just recently scientists have uncovered old graves, (in Iceland or Greenland, I believe), that showed the people had inner-breeded so much that the bones in the graves were deformed. Why?

Because new DNA from other places could not travel to Iceland or Greenland. So they inner-married with people related to one another. This is no different than what is presently happening in the world today.

As per God in His Master plan, the intelligence part in one parent's DNA develops, it brought forth knowledge within all DNA that follows.

We must go back to the Bible story of Adam and Eve once again. The story of Eden, is the explanation of humans learning the difference between right and evil. Yes, God did create evil because the act of evil was needed for humans to be able to judge their actions. The knowledge of judging the differences of right and wrong turned evil and polluted the thoughts of Eve, and caused her to look inward to her wants instead of seeing how her knowledge could help others. Corrupted thoughts of Eve made her teach her husband, Adam, how to obtain more. Once self-desires had set in his heart, Adam too, assumed that all others in their tribe knew he had more, and he refused to share his wealth and knowledge for the good of all. Therefore, Adam decided to leave the land of "Eden," and work virgin land elsewhere.

Years after leaving and working their farm, they had two sons. Their oldest son Cain became a farmer while their youngest son Abel became a shepherd. Cain was more like his mother than Abel, and he wanted to have everything that Abel had. Therefore, in anger, he murdered Abel. When Cain realized that his mother and father would find out what he had done, he left, but he was in fear that all the people in the world would also know what he had done. His fear caused him to create his god that said, "Whoever harms Cain, will receive seven times worse than what they did to him."

And the Bible story continues today. And thus is where the story of the curse came from.

16

The new things that we learn will be attached to our DNA, and that will be placed into our offspring when we procreate life. You see, you must examine the whole ball of string to understand life and why people act and react to certain situations as they do. One cannot pull out one single strand and obtain the knowledge of understanding life.

Peer Pressure

Peer pressure does not merely come from friends and other humans because it can come from family members as well as the other people "In the Know"... the clergy. They, the preachers, place their concepts upon us but they never will tell you all that they think but only what they have been taught. A prime example of this is say your preacher is talking to you about creation. He tells you, as it says in the Bible, that God created the earth in seven days. And you are thinking, such as I, also, how amazing God is.

But if your preacher truly believed in his Religion, he would not be over weight or doing things against his Religion or God. I know that most Religions state that obesity is a Sin. Is your minister committing a Sin by being fat?

Then you ask that dreaded question, "Who created God?"

(Children are great at asking this question and preachers are great at side stepping it. Why?)

Because no one has ever given them the answer, but only the best ways to side-step the question.

These are the things that our families try to enforce upon us; these things come from the dog that dwells within them. And those concepts may not have come along from friends but instead came from their DNA, the things that their ancestors learned or were taught that they felt were right for them.

Twins do not have to look alike nor do they have to act the same because of all the things that are engraved upon their DNA that came from their ancestors. Therefore, twins can act or look differently, and many times we will see siblings acting or looking differently, too.

An example; a grandparent may have been more religious than their children, where the grandchildren could be more religious than their parents, the grandparent's children. As in the story of how

David's cousin and he looked the same and acted similar; his father and his cousin's mother, his father's sister, did not look or act similar.

A high school teacher once told our older son, that the Moon produces its own light, (it is not reflected light from the Sun.) A silly comment from a confuse person.

Another high school teacher asked our youngest son, "What state touches both the Atlantic and Pacific Oceans?"

When our son said he didn't know the answer, she replied, "Florida."

Our son replied, "Florida does not touch two oceans, but only the Atlantic and the Gulf of Mexico."

The teacher said she would have to look in to that. She never told him or her class any different.

But sometimes, the teachers only teach what they were taught or what they thought was the truth. Or did that concept of the teacher come from their ancestors?

We only learn what our teachers claim is true.

Once while working as a truck mechanic in North Hollywood, California, David had lunch with a truck driver. As they ate, they talked about our up coming vacation. David told him that his family and he were driving back to visit his wife's brother in Virginia. He looked kind-of funny at David and asked, "Is Virginia on the other side of Texas?"

The truck driver did not know!

He was a truck driver who drove and traveled around the western states. We only learn and know what is needed by us.

We should not judge others but we must decide (judge) if their actions are right for us because those things we have placed upon our DNA will be carried onto our offspring.

Whereas, were the truck driver's concepts right for David? No way!

David did not judge him. David judged if his concepts of the United States were right for him.

The things that others believe may have come from their DNA, these strands on their DNA, may not have been dominate upon their parents. They may have lain dormant on their DNA until they were needed.

(After one dies, their family and friends usually have some type of wake; the family members have something to remember of the deceased that keeps the people together. This get together is for bringing the family members together as one again; to keep people in contact with each other, and to forget things that kept them apart. But usually after the deceased is laid to rest, the people will go back living in those ruts, the life style, in which they lived before.)

We as humans, are pleased when we find that others like the same things that we do. And we are happy when we discover a religion that worships the God that likes what we do. For surely, if another thinks as we than we must be right.

The human is a lazy animal and does not like to change concepts in life and does not like to discover that he was wrong, and he is willing to fight and even to die for his concepts.

When John Kennedy was alive and President, the Russian Prime Minister Khrushchev, stood up and said, "We do not need to fight the Americans, leave them alone and someday they will become Communist."

Today, we are becoming a Communist Country with our actions of the people that do not have concepts except those concepts from the majority. We are coming to the day, when the government rules that all people will have disaster insurance that will be paid by with income tax. And if the people cannot afford the income tax, the government will carry them.

We are heading to a world that there will not be any money; our governments will tell us where to work, where to live, who to marry, how many children we will have and what to eat; our governments will own everything… including us.

God created people in His image. And in His image, He is the center of His universe, and that is how all humans perceive our world to be. God is conscious of all His Angels and humans, and that is what we need to be. Jesus was put here on earth to demonstrate how we were supposed to live with each other, but we did not get it.

An old woman once said, "What is right is right and what is wrong is nobody."

Every person believes he is right and everyone else is wrong because no one thinks that he is wrong. Hence, nobody is wrong.

When a person tries to influence you with their thoughts, they are saying that they know better than you and you are wrong. But everyone is confused. No one knows everything, but everyone believes that he is right about everything.

But in God's Master plan of Creation, we are allowed to judge if the concepts of others are correct for us. By challenging the concepts of others we are raising the intelligence in the congregation of humanity. And that is a gift from the Creator – God.

Going with the Flow of Life

Everything that happens today was caused to happen from the actions of our ancestors in the past and all that happens was known to happen by God when He first created this reality.

The things that occurred in your ancestors lives influence you today. And those things play upon your likes and dislikes of today, and that is where your understanding of going with the flow of life first comes from.

I had told David an interesting story about my paternal grandmother. She was very close to me. My grandmother was born in the Middle East. When my grandmother, Dorthy, was very young, things were beginning to get bad in her homeland. Dorthy's family was of Christian faith. The Muslim's were beginning to rise up and force everyone to convert or be killed. Because she was the youngest, Dorthy's family thought that they could save her by sending her to America. They found a sponsor and at the age of almost fifteen years old, Dorthy found herself on a ship, heading for the United States of America, all by herself. I said she was so afraid, but always thought of my grandmother as being a very brave sole to take that trip alone, leaving everyone and everything she loved behind. Dorthy never saw any of her family again.

Once Dorthy was here in America, her sponsor took her in. However, she was never given an opportunity to continue her education. Not long after she arrived in this country, Dorthy met and fell in love with my grandfather, Ed. I am not sure how or where they met, only that not long after they first met they were married. I never knew of any paternal aunts or uncles.

I remember sitting with my grandmother with a Dr. Souse book and teaching her to read. Other times I recalled my grandmother sitting in a chair on the front lawn and just staring out at the blue sky and smiling. My grandmother loved being out doors. She loved the flowers, the trees, and the birds, just everything.

Years later, after my grandmother's death, I was talking to a cousin and asked him if he had ever heard of any paternal aunts or uncles from our grandfather's side. He told me that grandma and grandpa actually only had each other because everyone disowned them. You see, my paternal grandfather was Pennsylvania Dutch and his family would not accept him marrying outside of their culture. At the same time, my grandmother's sponsors would not accept her marrying anyone outside of their culture, which was Arabic. Therefore, Dorthy and Ed lived their life together and raised their children together. They were their only family. I thought it to be so sad that my grandparents had no family to share their life with. They were going with the flow of life. Even though both sides of the family disowned Dorthy and Ed, their DNA will live forever through them and their children.

The design of our DNA, all that is recorded upon our DNA, is directed by the way our ancestors viewed life back in the past. The things that our ancestors did may have been correct for them but may not be correct of us today. Our life styles of today could be completely different than our ancestors because of all that other people, our peers, force upon us.

David was born in 1944, and the 60s and early 70s were his years. He was young and in the prime of life. He was strong and knew everything, and life was his. David did not think about what was right or wrong but only of things that concerned him. And those things were from what he had learned from peers and his family. Even his reasoning that told him who was sane or insane came from his concepts and those, his concepts, came from his DNA.

Another great example of this is our views of government today; we believe that our government is correct because of the world that we live in today; those that lost the wars in the past, we believe were fighting for the wrong reasons. We have been taught to believe that the concepts of our ancestors were correct about everything that they did, even their reasoning has been placed upon our DNA.

Each of us, including our siblings, may have different concepts.

This occurs because an individual's concepts comes from what is dominate upon that individual's DNA, even though the same DNA came from the same parents, and their DNA concepts changed through the years that they lived. But even a twins DNA concepts may vary because the individual's DNA contains different traits from any one or more of his ancestors, and therefore, those traits could be different than his twin.

When one is selecting a mate, one must examine who were the parents of the selected mate's DNA. That is no different than finding a mate who will strengthen your offspring; will the health of that fat person who you enjoyed procreating with be up to what you expect it to be in later life?

Is their life-style the way that you expect your life and your children to be?

Are they willing to work for the kinds of earthly goods that you want?

What and how will they teach their children?

Before, David thought going with the flow of life meant to go with the business (jobs) and money flow of life. Because back then, he was always broke and fighting to get ahead in the world, and he found out that style of life works; just relax and let life go on and you would eventually come ahead in life.

But now, he thinks of how long life will last. When you are young, you only think of how sweet life is and how you will change it. As you become older, you realize life has a beginning, middle and an ending. At 63 years old, David realizes that life was programmed with a clock built into it. Our ancestors had length in their lives, and that length of life was engraved into David's DNA. He now is over his youth and in middle age, God did not promise him a long life, all He promised David was a life that he could experience. David cannot demand Him, he will live a long life or will die this year or the next. All that he can do is enjoy life and have fun in the years that he has left, but surely he will die someday. Therefore, all that he has left is how he will enjoy life that remains in his body. Because now he realizes that the statement, "Go with the Flow of Life," is capitalized. Going with the Flow means; All Life.

Do not be afraid of death. Humans do not have the intelligence to sustain life. The doctors practice to try to extend our lives with experimental drugs and procedures, but the intelligence to sustain a real quality of life is just not there.

Do not allow evil to grow within yourself?

The actions, things that others do is not your concern. Allow others to do what is right for them. Judge others actions to see if their actions are correct for you. But do not judge the other person.

When life is gone, your life is gone, because life will continue on for others but without you, just as life has continued on without the people who died before. Their concepts of things that they disliked or liked died with them, but those concepts may continue to live with others. But did their death not change what would happen in the future?

Does your hating another change what happens after you die?

It may, if your concepts are believed by others. But for sure, the world will continue without you; it does not matter what you thought, and therefore, it does not really matter what happens now.

Just walk through a graveyard and view the graves of those who have died before. It does not matter if they lived last year or one hundred years earlier, they are gone. God did not promise them that they would live forever. Why do you think that you were special and would live forever?

God did not promise your parents that they would live one thousand years, and He did not promise you that all the people that you knew would live forever.

David asked two people, "Is all known by God?'

The first person answered, "No."

And David replied, "It is absurd to believe that God would allow the Bible to be written incorrectly. He would not allow falsehoods to be placed into the future of His world, but people of then wrote in their knowledge and used the language of that day. Therefore, the Bible may have been written using the world's words. But you believe God did not know what was going to be written to His Christian Bible, are you saying that the Bible may be wrong?

Including what is written into St. John's Revelations?"

He did not answer.

The second man that David talked about God's knowledge, answered, "If God knows all, then I should sit here and do nothing."

David answered, "God knows everything, but you do not know what you will think or how you will react to your actions. And that is the reason for life, for you to know how you will react. How an individual acts from situations is one of the gifts from God. Yes, God does know what will occur and happen, but the action is left up to the individual. Because what will happen and cause the reactions was known by God when He first implanted intelligence into the first one-cell animal that moved upon the earth. And if you sit here and do nothing, that, too, was known by God."

He too, did not have an answer.

We must think outside of life in attempting to understand life. All life is connected to previous life, and therefore, all life has influenced life.

Many times, we do not allow ourselves to think or do things because of others; we don't like being different from others. Or because we don't want others to confront us on our concepts. But when life is gone, they or you won't be here. So are you allowing another person to control you in where and with whom you want to be near?

This location in this time will never occur again, and by you not being here, you are allowing the concepts of another to influence you. That is the same as telling people that the other person is correct and you are wrong.

You will never be able to go back in time to be with and see the people that you wanted to be with. Are you going to allow another to dominate you and tell you where not be be?

David and I first met in the spring of 1975, and by November 12th of 1975, we were married. My father did not want me marrying any one especially David. Because of my father's concepts, during the first few years, we did not have anything to do with my family or him. Now he is dead, but for a few of the years that followed, My mother was alone. We did become friends with her again, but not with all of my siblings. Some of them still carried their father's, Joey's, concepts within them. During the late summer of 2007, at my mother's funeral, only one of my siblings talked with David. They still carry their daddy's hatred within.

When Joey was alive, David and I should not have cared about what he thought, we should have been friends with my siblings anyway. We should have visited with them, he should not have caused us to stay away from my family. And now it's too late to go back and change the past because that time is gone forever.

What others think is not your concern. If you wish to be near someone, be there. Do what is best for you. Allow others to be free as you.

You only live once and you will never live again; life is not a dress rehearsal for another life that will follow this one.

Be with the friends and people that you wish to be with before it's too late.

Entities

Entities are around all of us in our daily lives, and those Entities are the deceased from our past. Life is merely the middle page of life. And the Entities are there to help us in creating our Souls, that should be for God, but our lives, whatever we endured, is part of His Master plan.

David, was born and raised in Wooster, Ohio, and as he recalled, he lived across the street from a Nazarene Church. On Wednesdays, he liked sitting outside on the warm summer evenings and listening to the people in the church sing of praise to God.

One Sunday morning as the church let out, he was playing with some neighbor kids, as he ran he fell forward onto his face with a small metal ladder in his mouth. The toy ladder cut him under his tongue and as he got up and cried with blood running from his mouth onto his shirt, all the church people looked at him and laughed. Another Sunday morning, as the adults stood and talked with their preacher outside and in front of this Nazarene Church, their kids threw stones at the birds in the middle of the street. One of the boys hit a bird with a rock and as the little bird lay there flopping his wings, the boy told his parents and their preacher, and they started laughing at the bird. No one cared about the injured little bird...but David did.

If children and their parents and their preachers (people) did not follow or learn anything from what they were taught in Church, then could it be the truth?

When David was six years old, his mother went shopping and his older sister watched David and her other younger siblings. It was in the fall, and David and his siblings went outside to play in the cold rain. When their mother returned home, she gave his sister heck for allowing them to play outside. As David became sick with a cold, he remembered looking out their kitchen window and seeing the leaves falling off the trees. His cold turned into pneumonia, and he lay on their couch when the doctor came and visited with him daily. They didn't have enough beds and had to sleep on the floor. His parents gave him an early Christmas because the doctor told them that he may not live through the winter. David remembers being so sick that he would fly to the Other Side and play along the wall there, and he was always looking for someone who he never found.

The next thing that he remembers, he was weak and standing looking out their kitchen window again, all of the snow was gone and it was now spring and all the new green leaves were sprouting on the trees. Of course, he failed that first grade of school and, also, his third grade because of pneumonia again.

As a young child, David was always surrounded by "Ghost". Back then, he always thought of Entities as "Ghost".

He remembers seeing a little short haired white and brown dog running on the stairs in the other side of his families duplex house, the little dog stopped at the top of the stairs, looked back at him and then disappeared.

As a young child, David remembers seeing a horse drinking at a watering trough, when he ran out to get a closer look at the horse, it was gone.

(Children are afraid of seeing Entities or ghost; entities may appear as animals so that people do not become afraid.)

Entities can and do come back as animals, but animals do not have Souls as humans do. And animals will never live forever as a part in God's Master plan. David's seeing the ghostly animals was the first days of God's Angels coming into contact with him, that he knows of. Because back then and after the incidents that happened at the church across from where he was born and grew up at caused him to say, "I will not kneel down for God or the Devil…I will just stay here on Earth forever."

But the Entities were trying to get his attention throughout his life.

Besides all that they showed him in his younger years, they had to teach him and wait until he was ready. And that was not until he met Joan Lee Harris in the summer of 1965.

And it was her, her Entity after her death in the fall of 1968, that he would trust and believe in. She was the only person, living or dead, that could tell him and teach him of God.

David's dad told him a story about when they were fishing late one night. His dad looked around at him laying on the ground sleeping by their fire, and behind David stood a man dressed in a hooded black robe. His dad never said anything more about what he saw that night.

One night, after late evening fishing, as one of David's older brothers drove them home in his car, the fog was heavy as they drove slowly following an old wagon down the highway, as they approached a railroad crossing the wagon disappeared. All of his family members in the car saw the wagon and they all saw the wagon disappear, and they all talked about how strange that was.

David also recalls the winter night that his older brothers were in Akron, playing music, and the snow was falling heavily. His mother and he sat in their kitchen and talked. They heard someone, his older brother Frank, walk across their porch and stop at the kitchen door, but never came in. David and his mother both got up and went to the kitchen door and opened it, but no one was there. There were no foot prints in the newly fallen snow. The next day, after his brothers returned home, Frank, one of David brothers, said that he wanted to come home that night but they stayed in Akron until the next morning when the snow let up.

As David became older and worked in the oil fields of Ohio, one evening he saw someone standing and looking at some of their equipment and walked around behind it. David ran out there looking for that person. There was no one to be found, he had vanished. Later David learned that the man that he had seen, died weeks before when he fell 60 foot to his death from the drilling rig derrick.

My paternal grandmother told me about one night as she and my parents were sitting in the kitchen of their home in Norton, Ohio, which my grandfather had built, having coffee and talking. The kitchen light fixture was a round, tubular fluorescent light. All of a sudden, the kitchen light went dim and their was a blue light that just kept circling the fixture over and over again for what seemed to be forever. Then my grandmother said that it was probably only a couple of minutes, but it seemed to be forever. Soon the light became bright again and no one said a word. My grandmother told me that she just knew that it was my grandfather that was circling the light that night.

I can also recall a cold winter night not long after my family had moved to Newcomerstown, Ohio. We lived on a farm about three miles outside of town. The driveway to the farm had about a steep 45 degree angle. My father was disabled at the time and could not get out of bed, let alone walk. In the middle of the night, all of a sudden my father jumped up out of bed and ran out of the house and ran straight up the driveway. By the time my mother and brothers caught up to him, he was collapsed at the top of the driveway. He told them he saw a bright light and was following it. He wanted to go with it because his father was there.

When David and I were married, David's brother, Dean, his wife of then, now they are divorced, told me about the day that David's mother along with her and Dean had seen Jody, a deceased sister-in-law; they heard and seen Jody walking across the porch to the kitchen door and then disappear.

Then after David's and my son, Tony was born, and just before we moved to California, we lived a month with David's family. Tony would tell us about playing with Jody. He never knew her because she died years before he was born.

We moved to California because of our dear and close friend, Jimmy Bryant. He was the person that produced me on my first records on his label. We came to California because he was planning to record me and Rex Allen Jr. on an album, but his lung cancer became worse, he was dying. Twice, I talked with him after he had died.

(He always liked talking to people on the phone when he was alive.)

The first time I talked with Jimmy, I could not remember much about our conversation. But the second time was different, we went to bed, the telephone rang and I woke up and sat up on the side of the bed. All he said was, "Everything is okay, be happy in life." I then realized that I was awake and sitting on the edge of our bed and talking with Jimmy, but by then, he was gone and the telephone went dead.

After moving to California, we bought our first house in Granada Hills, California.

It was strange the way things always seemed to start acting up in the fall. We had moved into this house a week before Thanksgiving in 1981. Tony was only five years old at the time. The first night in the house did not go without incident. We woke the following morning to find all the lights in the front of the house on. At first, we thought that maybe Tony had turned them on. But there was no way he could have reached the light switch in the kitchen located above the stove.

Many times we heard the pitter patter of little feet running in the hall during the night. Our house had hardwood floors, no carpet anywhere. We thought it was Tony, but David or I would get up to find Tony sound asleep in his room and the rest of the house was very cold and silent.

I recalled the incident with the big velvet painting.

I had it hanging in the living room above the Elgin Pendulum stand that held a house plant on top of it.

When we got home from work that day, we found the painting had been removed from the wall and carefully placed behind the door that led to the back hallway. Immediately, thinking our house had been broken into, we checked all the doors and windows. Everything was still locked. Nothing was missing from within the house. No one had broken in.

The picture did not just fall off the wall and then bounce over behind the door because the Elgin Pendulum and the plant that was directly under the picture were not damaged.

When Tony was about seven years old, he had a pretend friend named Peter, whom he said lived in his closet. Tony was always playing with his friend and talking to him.

I was not sure if it was Peter, but I remembered Tony telling us that while he was in his room he saw a boy standing in the hall.

The boy told Tony, "I gotta go now."

Then he turned, walked down the hall and disappeared.

There was also the pot roast that disappeared.

I had set out a roast for dinner.

I remembered that we got into some kind of argument about the roast. For some reason David did not want it, but I cannot remember why.

For some strange reason, the roast just disappeared. We looked everywhere for it, but never did find it.

Many times we could hear aircraft communications on radios that were turned off.

Before David's mom died, she had come to visit us in 1982.

She slept in the guest room. This was not the first time she had come to stay with us, but for some reason, after the first few nights, she had asked us if it would be alright if she left her light on all night. She never told us why or what had happened.

After David's mom had passed away, Dianna, our daughter who was killed in a car accident years later, had told us about talking to her grandmother, Dave's Mom, on the phone.

Many mornings we woke to find the sliding patio door unlocked, yet the pole that was placed across the bottom of the door for security had not been removed. And there were many days we would come home from work or from one of Tony's baseball games and we would find the same thing.

When Dan was born, he was a very sick baby.

The doctors could not find what was wrong with our son. He just seemed to be in pain a lot of the time. Dan would want us to pick him up, but it seemed to hurt him when we did.

I remembered one night when we didn't know what to do. Dan cried and cried. I laid him down on to the couch. Dan got a dazed look on his face. He was no longer crying.

I became very upset and wanted to call the doctor.

David told me not to. He told me that Dan was okay. He said that he knew Dan was flying and had left his body. David reminded me of the times when he was little and very sick and left his body to escape the pain. And that he remembered sleeping and leaving his body and flying on the Other Side at a place he used to play at before he was born.

Within a few minutes, Dan was back and no longer crying. He was his playful self again.

When Dan was about two or three, he was sitting on the love seat in the living room watching television. David and I were sitting just outside the patio door where we were only a few feet from him. Suddenly, Dan began to cry, repeating, "Stop it! Stop it!"

We looked in at Dan and saw his little head bobbing back and forth as if someone were pushing it.

We rushed inside. Dan cried and wanted to be held. I picked him up and comforted him.

I often wondered about the old Sea Captain that I had seen in the backyard while hanging laundry.

This ghostly old gent wore a captain style cap and a dark blue coat. One arm hung by his side while his other hand was in his coat pocket. He just looked at me, then vanished. I had seen him a couple times, and I refused to go back out there after dark again.

It was about that time when Dan was around three or four years old that he recalls even today, about how his grandmother, David's deceased mother, would lift him up and place him on the swing in our backyard.

Then there was the ball.

On three different occasions, I had told David about a colorful light in the shape of a ball that I had seen in my rearview mirror as I drove. I had told him that the colors were the basic colors. The top edge was sort of a whitish yellow that turned into orange and the bottom part was red.

At first, I thought it was some kind of a reflection from the sun, but even when I would make a turn and head in a different direction, the ball remained in the same spot. It always disappeared when I got home. This happened while we lived in Granada Hills; once in our Toyota Landcruiser and once in our GMC Van. The third incident occurred when I was driving home from work to our home in Lancaster in my Chrysler New Yorker.

But that third time was a little different.

The inside of my car became deathly cold and its windows began to frost over, and its electronic instruments quit working. Then a few miles from home, everything went back to normal. I was never so afraid in my life.

I could not remember exactly when the elephant sounds started, but all of us kept hearing it.

One night the yelling continued so much, David finally shouted, "Shut up, I need to get some sleep."

He rolled over away from the noisy elephant sound and immediately he felt a warm little hand on his bare shoulder as if it were trying to pull him back over.

A few times David told me of hearing this strange elephant sound going deep into his ear as though it were entering his brain.

A PHD Physicist friend told David in a phone conversation, if he could record it then it was real. He did record the strange elephant sound as well as other sounds.

Then there was the night that I woke up and found David screaming in a woman's voice.

I cannot remember what the voice was saying, but I do remember how scared I was.

There was also an incident about a phone call David was suppose to have made to his brother, Phil, who was near death because of lung cancer.

Phil and David never got along and had not spoken to each other in a long time.

Yet, after Phil's death, his other brothers thanked David for calling Phil just before his end.

They said that before David called, Phil was in a lot of pain. Phil never told them what he and David talked about, but his pains were eased after he hung up the phone.

David knew that he never called Phil, "To Hell with the bastard," is what he thought. "Rot in Hell!" was how he cared about Phil.

There was also a strange whistling that would be heard throughout the house. This whistling would occur night or day. We would run from room to room trying to find its source, which we never did find.

There was another time when David had a bad toothache. Nothing would help.

He remembered taking different kinds of pain pills and toothache medicine and finally, he laid down and said, "It's now or never!"

When he awoke the next morning, his toothache was gone.

I told me how he had walked the floors all night long, but he swore that he slept all night and he recalled feeling very rested, as though he had had a good nights sleep.

When we decided to sell, with the house on the market for sale, I recalled two perspective buyers and the realtor telling us that they saw two Entities walk through a wall. The realtor refused to handle the house and canceled their contract. David and I were able to find another realtor that sold our house within two weeks.

After the house was finally sold, David, Tony, and Dan had taken a load of furniture to storage and I was getting the last bit of our things ready for storage. All of a sudden, in a crackling voice, I heard a tiny soft voice say, "I… go… too?"

I did not know what to do or say. I felt sad inside and very sorry for the thing. Dave and the boys also felt the same way about the Entity.

It was also strange that we never had any problems for the three months that we lived in our motor home in Castaic after we sold our home. We were supposed to be there for only two weeks, but our new home in Palmdale was not completed until the end of March.

Right after moving to Palmdale, California, things were not right as with the unexplained high electric bills. Though our house was large and had a pool and spa, our electric bills were high enough for two homes.

David had some knowledge of electricity, so he checked out the amperage use of the pump motors plus all other electric appliances in our house. It did not add up to the amount of electric we were using.

I even thought that maybe our neighbor's house was wired through our meter. The electric company came out and checked our meter. Everything looked okay. No reason was ever found for the enormous electrical usage.

One evening in early 1990, Dianna called and talked with me for a very long time then she wanted to talk with David. They talked for over an hour. David felt strange about that conversation, it was like she had to make sure that he knew that she loved him…kind-of like she thought he was going to die. Within a few days later, we received the phone call that she died. We flew back to Ohio for her funeral.

As we walked up to her casket to see her for the last time, our youngest son, Dan, held a little Lego man that he had been playing with. David took the Lego man and placed him into his pocket. Staring down at Dianna, he needed something to send with her…something that showed that we still loved her… he couldn't send her away without something. With his hand in his pocket, he felt the little Lego man; he placed him in the casket with Dianna.

After we arrived home in California, we found the little Lego man on our counsel , the engine cover, in our van. The same Lego man that he left with Dianna in her casket.

That Lego man now stands on our dresser in our bedroom today.

It reminds us of the love that we had and have for Dianna.

Jewelry, which David had bought for me in Spain that had disappeared several years prior now reappeared on my dresser.

Still friends told David, Tony and I that they had called and left messages with some old woman. No old woman lived with us.

One night after going to bed, Dan screamed.

David and I ran into his bedroom.

Dan was crying, stating that something just hit the wall over his head.

We looked and saw that just inches above him there was a hammer like impression in the wall. It seemed like Dan was bothered more than the rest of our family by these unusual happenings.

One school Holiday while David and I were at work, Dan was having problems with the ghost again.

Tony was walking into Dan's room, telling Dan that there are no ghost, and something hit Tony on his chin, "like a fist," and knocked him against the wall.

Day or night, you could hear people walking around upstairs in the attic. Sometimes you would hear water being run or a toilet being flushed and you might hear chains rattling up there, too.

Many times we heard doors opening and closing. More than once when we came home we found TVs and/or radios turned on.

One of our last Christmas' spent in our Palmdale home, after days of endless noises and seeing things, everyone was so afraid that we all slept in the family room for four nights and we left all the lights on in the house. On a morning of one of those days, we found on the floor of our "bedroom" a jeweled cross that was all bent up. This jeweled cross belonged to me and I kept it in my jewelry box upstairs, but the cross was not bent before.

Sometimes as we sat in our back yard enjoying our pool or spa, we would look up and see someone walk past the window of our upstairs master bedroom.

Now I can laugh about that night that we got so mad at the happenings in our house that David and I actually went into Dan's bedroom and David cussed out this ghost. He gave it a good old oil field cussing as we heard it shifting its weight from one foot to the other in Tony's bedroom. The creaking of the floor made it sound very heavy. He demanded it to fight him. The thing never did, and I was kind of glad that it did not accept his challenge.

One afternoon, the smell of roses filled the house. David and I raced from room to room trying to find out where the smell was coming from. In the kitchen, in an area of about a three foot circle, the rose smell was the strongest. It was so strong that the smell was sickening. It lasted for about one half hour before the odor disappeared.

We all used to laugh while watching our little pet dog as he would look around the room as if he were watching someone or something fly around. We laughed at him until we once saw him fly across the room and land on the couch.

One night, David and I lay in bed and we could hear someone walking in the attic above. The next morning, in our walk-in closet we found the lid to the attic was twisted like it had been opened.

On another night, David waited for me to come to bed. All of the lights were turned off and the street light shown on the wall. Then all of a sudden writing appeared on the wall. He was unable to figure out what it said before it disappeared.

David was not sure if he saw the eyes the same night he saw the writing on the wall. The incident with the eyes was similar to the writing. While David waited for me, he saw two large red eyes appear on the ceiling of our bedroom. The eyes appearance lasted for a few minutes then they were gone.

One of Tony's girl friends, Lisa, told a strange story, the same story that David's sister had told him and I years before.

Lisa was sleeping in her room, and all at once she woke up.

A round ball was on her wall that was the same colors of the ball that had ridden in the cars with me.

David was missing. No one knew where he was. Lisa and I cried because we were worried about David. A little ghost appeared and told us he knew where David was and that he would take me to him. I refused out of fear but Lisa said she would go with him.

Hand-in-hand, the ghost and Lisa entered the ball of light on the wall.

They flew over a house that Lisa did not know. In the side yard, stood a group of people looking at a crack in a step to the back door of this house, near them David lay dead. Not one of the people cared about him.

Lisa had described David's mother's house. Those were his brothers and sisters she had seen. She had described a house and people that she had never seen or met before. Lisa knew and told exactly the same story that David's sister had told us years prior, but she never met his sister. Tony couldn't have told Lisa this story because he had never heard this story before. How did Lisa know the story unless it really happened to her?

David knew his brothers and sisters did not care for him. Out of eleven kids, I kept in touch with two sisters. The rest of his family were like strangers to us.

His family troubles stemmed from his brother Phil. Phil could have been a good brother except in his younger days he listened to what everyone said; their older brothers talked him into quitting school to play music in their band. He never worked at any other kind of job. He never had a girl friend that David knew of, and he never moved out of their parents' home.

Their mother would carry meals up to Phil's room. He didn't want anyone to see him. His teeth rotted out and he grew thin. He bragged he only needed to use a cigarette lighter once in the morning and then he chained smoked the rest of the day. He kept a loaded shotgun next to his bed. They claimed he would kill and had threatened all of his brothers and sisters.

David tried to get Phil professional help, but their mom kept saying there was nothing wrong with Phil. Phil ruled and controlled their mother and father. He destroyed any relationship that David could have had with their parents.

The last ten years or so that Phil lived, he demanded money from their mom, and she gave him all he wanted.

Phil died in Buffalo, New York, at a hospital on Halloween from lung cancer at the age of forty-nine.

Phil was one of the reasons that David left home and joined the Army. Was there any wonder why even today he still dislikes Phil.

After Phil's death, their mother stated that she communicated with Phil many times; she would ask him questions and he would answer by knocking on the bathroom wall.

Many other strange things happened when we lived in Palmdale, too.

While working the graveyard shift for a pharmaceutical company one of these Entities went to work with David.

The ghost whistled at him from in the locked maintenance shop. David ran around and looked for who ever whistled, no one could be found.

Another night, one of the workers, while sizing vitamins, looked up to see an old woman standing and staring at him. The building had security with closed circuit TV. No one could have entered the building without being seen. Security searched everywhere for the old woman. They never found her, and the guy quit his job immediately.

While doing apartment maintenance, an Entity once again went to work with David. The assistant manager saw the old sea captain outside her window one night. She described the same sea captain that I had seen in Granada Hills, but the assistant manager lived on the second floor.

The manager of the apartments and David were going to check out a vacant apartment. She tried to open the door, the door was pushed shut from the inside. Again she tried to open the door, this time the door opened. They both ran inside and looked for whoever shut the door. No one was there. The windows were closed and they all had screens on them. Again, this apartment was on the second floor.

Late one night, David was driving home on the freeway when the car filled with the smell of beer. The odor only lasted a few minutes and then was gone. He had quit drinking years before and no beer was ever carried in this car, but the car was once owned by a departed friend that drank heavily when alive.

It was around this time that an assistant preacher that lived near us told us that many times, he had seen people who owned or were given used wood or cloths that contained Entities. He suggested that we get rid of all old things in our home. After weeks of throwing away many objects, we found out that the first house we owned, a friend of ours had given us a used blanket that came from his apartment. His apartment had a recent owner who died while lying on that blanket. We placed the blanket in a garbage bag and placed it outside. That night, there was knocking on our door, but no one was there. The next day, David took the trash bag to the dump. And we never had anymore bad Entities after that.

But things didn't get much better after moving into Lancaster, California.

I remember things that Tony had told us about, such as pennies flying off of his desk and landing beside him on his bed.

Unlike Dan, Tony would take these things in stride and tried not to let them scare him.

Either that or he didn't want me to know how afraid he was.

David remembers Tony telling him about going on a date one night. His girlfriend was complaining that it was cold in the car so Tony turned the heater on. He kept it on high, but the car just would not warm up the way it normally did. He looked into his rearview mirror and saw his grandmother, David's mom, who had passed away seven years earlier, sitting in the back seat.

On another occasion, Tony was in his room doing something and he saw his grandmother again. This time, she was sitting in the easy chair in his room, she sat there as she did in the car, looking straight ahead and never said anything. But as an Entity she never talked to Tony.

And then, about a year or so later, Tony was home alone. Our little dog ran into the dining room barking. The little dog stopped barking and sat down, looking up and started wagging his tail about five feet from a corner of the room. Tony walked over to the dog and bent down to pick him up. As Tony stood up holding the dog, he saw his deceased grandfather, David's dad, standing in front of him.

The smoke like Entity said, "Do not be afraid," and disappeared.

David's dad had died fourteen months after his mom had passed away. Tony was very close to both of his grandparents.

As it says in the Christian Bible, "If you see an Entity, just ask if they are of God and they must answer."

The true answer is; if they are of God, they will answer; if they do not and cannot answer then they are of Evil.

David's mother and Phil could not answer, but his father could. Therefore, his mom and Phil were not of God, while his dad was of God.

As David and I spoke about Entities being of God, I told him another incident with my paternal grandparents. I never knew my grandfather as he died before I was ever born. I told David how my grandmother would always talk to my deceased grandfather. She would say things like, "Ed, this is Christine, your granddaughter." and then she would start telling him all about me and what we were doing. I would look around the room and be confused because there was no one there. At a young age, I did not realize who Ed was. My grandmother would tell me that he was there, but he just could not answer her but she was sure that he could hear her. Today it makes me wonder if he could not answer her because he was not of God.

After David and I were married, I kept seeing my grandmother in my dreams. I missed her so much, but I just could not understand what she was trying to tell me. Finally, David put me under hypnosis. My grandmother was telling me about the post bank that my grandfather had. Back in those days, people did not always trust putting their money into the bank. My grandfather actually put his money in one of the post holes in the fence around their home he built in Norton, Ohio. After David put me under hypnosis, I never had those recurring dreams of my grandmother again.

A few years ago, we took a trip back to Ohio and decided to go to Norton to the old homestead. The house is now gone and the land is a big nursery. We decided to just let it go, we really don't need the money now.

And there were a few times that Tony came home to find his room tore up. Things would be thrown and scattered everywhere.

Then there was Dan.

He seemed to be more prone to strange occurrences than Tony.

He always slept with his light on and did not like to be alone for very long. In fact, Dan always liked to be where he could see someone at all times.

He had seen Entities all over the house. He had seen them walking up and down the stairs. He even had gone into the garage and seen one sitting in one of the cars. Dan had told his dad, David, about these sightings several times.

One day Dan walked into the garage and our 1979 Mercedes Benz diesel automobile started up. Dan looked and no one was in the car. He turned and ran back into the house and the car turned off. He did not like to go into the garage unless someone went with him or he left the door from the house to the garage open.

Dan was very meticulous about where he put things and how he had them arranged. And many times he had gotten up in the mornings to find a lot of things in his room had been rearranged. And he had also seen things move by themselves in his room.

I recall how Dan would come running down stairs because one of his toys turned themselves around or moved across the room. Also there were times when Dan would be in bed and his little toy Gargoyles would shoot their suction cup darts at him.

More than once, Dan saw a woman dressed in white walk across the living room, down the hall and then vanish through the closed door to the master bedroom.

Once he stated that the Entity woman was sitting on our couch as he watched TV, a bee-bee flew across the room, she jumped up and blocked the bee-bee and it fell to the floor. He showed us where the carpet was burned as if a shoe print, where she stood up.

There were several other times when I was cleaning and would come across the same type of bee bees on the carpet. We also had oil paintings hanging on the walls. Some of the paintings mysteriously had bee bee holes in them with bee bees lodged into the walls behind them. I might add here that our boys never had bee bee guns. I thought they were too dangerous and was afraid they would get hurt.

I also saw the same woman, but this time the woman was standing near fireplace in our living room. I remembered that the woman was about five foot tall and was wearing a full skirted knee length white with some kind of blue floral print dress with short puffy sleeves. I thought that the woman may have been David's mother when she was younger. I thought that because I really did not know of any other woman that was that short and had passed on. When I described this woman to Tony and David, Tony exclaimed, "That's the same woman I saw in our house in Granada Hills when I was six years old."

We did not know it back then, but was the Angel Jo, carrying the Soul of Joan Lee Harris within her.

Not once in all these years did David ever see any ghost or Entities. He heard many strange noises but never saw anything.

Over the years, he had always said, he was studying these ghosts and he didn't want them to leave just yet.

He felt that he learned how they moved from room to room in

houses, traveling down electric wire like roads. David thought they lived in low electric like diodes or computer chips used in communication and other household appliances. Their reflections that we see is actually off the low end of our color spectrum, and they are really low levels of electric energy.

He thought over the years Entities had entered his mind to "live" his life. As they relived his daily routine,he thought that he was reliving their lives.

David could recall being upstairs in an old wooden house.

Suddenly he heard someone coming up the stairs. Panic struck him as he ran over and tried to hide inside of a wall. He could see cobwebs and dust that had settled on the harden plaster that oozed out between the wooden slats. I stood there still, hoping the human would not see me. A guy comes into the room and looked around. Not seeing anyone, he left David was relieved that he was not seen.

He could also recall flying with someone else; they are playing some sort of tag. He was being chased by this other person. Flying fast and hard, he slammed into the ground. Down into the earth he goes then he turned upward. All of a sudden he stopped and looked around. He was inside of a coffin. A dead man's forehead was pressed to the lid. The skin on his neck had pulled his mouth open, and some of the lining of the coffin was hanging down. The casket was cast in a bluish white light. The light was coming from David... he was glowing. He felt real sad about this old dead man. All of a sudden, the other Entity had caught-up to him. She was also sad about the man. After a moment they continue their game and fly away.

David also remembers flying straight up out of a house into the night sky, faster and faster. He flew straight up until he could see the complete Earth far below him. How beautiful the world and universe looked from there.

He had thought that he learned the experiences of these from Entities, but now he realized he was only remembering things that he had done.

AndI will never forget December 21, 1996. Our oldest son, Tony, his girlfriend was going out of town for Christmas, so we were having a little Christmas party with her before she left. Like most people, we took pictures of each other opening gifts.

After getting the pictures back a few days later, we found

something very interesting.

There was a group of three pictures taken in a row of Tony opening his gift from his girlfriend. In the first picture, on the left side, there was a whitish, smoke-swirled haze. In the second picture that was taken, there were four or five of these whitish, smoke-swirled hazes that resembled forms of people. In that picture, at the far left, that form resembled a woman. And in the last picture, part of the woman can be seen at the right side of the picture. The three pictures present a prognosis of the woman, the Angel Jo, herding other Entities through our living room.

David had told me many times that he wished he had taken a photo of Jo lee Harris when they were going together back in 1965. Did Jo grant him his wish and allow her picture to be taken?

Did she give him her photo as a Christmas Gift?

It is known among ghost hunters that Entities pictures can be taken, when using 35mm, high speed film such as 400 film. Entities look like whitish smoke on the picture. But if you take the negatives into a photo shop and they do a reverse negative of the photo, you will see the Entities.

"One night I left my body and traveled to the Light. On the Other Side, I saw a bright light in the distance. I am not sure if I was walking or floating or what, but I remember that as I approached the Light, I looked over my shoulder and saw David and the Angel Joleen. They looked at me and we smiled at each other. Then I went on into the Light. That vision was so real to me. I feel deep in my heart that when I die this is exactly what will happen. I will go into the Light. I will not stay outside of the Light with David and the other Angels."

I believe it was in 1998, a friend, Dale, sat in our living room as we all talked with the Angel Gabrael. Dale told us that he did not get along with his brother. Gabrael told Dale that his brother still carried Dale's picture in his wallet. Finally weeks later, Dale talked with his brother once again on the phone, and his brother stated that he indeed carried Dale's picture in his wallet.

During December of 1999, David and I decided to record a few Christmas Songs for my mother. In the studio all went good, but after all the musicians were gone, and David was laying down my final vocal track, we noticed someone was singing with her. No one but the engineer, David and I were in the studio, but there was a man singing with me…A man saying, "Drink, drink" behind my singing. We could not find where that man's voice came from but left it on the tracks.

It was on a Halloween evening of Trick or Treating, a family rang our door bell. We answered the door as the family yelled "Trick or Treat."

One of their little boys started to walk into our home, the boy's dad said, "Where do you think you are going?"

The little boy answered, "I'm going up to the loft and play with the rest of the kids up there," as he looked and pointed up at our loft.

He had seen the Entity children playing up there. At that time, we didn't have any children. Our children had grown up years earlier.

A friend told us the story of when her husband was in the hospital and he was in a coma. After many days of seeing him lifeless in bed, one day as she parked her car and walked into the hospital, she could not take it anymore and broke-down and cried. Not wanting her family seeing her in that condition, she decided to have a cup of coffee in the cafeteria first before going up to see her husband. The cafeteria was empty. She poured a cup of coffee and paid for it walked over and sat down at a table in the corner of the room. An older woman walked in alone. She got a cup of coffee and came to the table and asked if she could sit down, too.

Our friend thought that was a little strange because the dining room was empty, but she said okay anyway.

The elderly woman sat down. Their small talk turned to our friend's husband. The old woman reached across the table and touched our friend's arm and as she did this, the old woman said, "Its okay, everything will be okay."

Then they both got up and walked out of the cafeteria to the elevators together. The two women got into the elevator and our friend pushed the button for the floor she wanted and looked at the old woman as to say "What floor?"

The old woman said, "That's okay."

When the elevator reached their floor and as the door opened, our friend turned around towards the old woman, but she was gone. She never got out of the elevator, she just vanished. When our friend walked into her husband's room, she found him sitting up. He was no longer in the coma. Our friend never saw the old woman again.

David had a friend that for years had seen his two deceased brothers around. They never said a word, just stood there and looked at him. They were evil in life, but they were there to help him change the directions in his life. He continued to drink and was not a good person in his life. In the late summer of 2007, he died in a truck accident. He did not change his directions before his death. You decide if he went to Heaven or Hell.

In the summer of 2006, David was able to locate his brother who is three years older than him. In their telephone conversation, they talked about the "ghost" that haunted them as children. He stated that after David left their home, the "ghost" never bothered the rest of their family again.

Now God's Angels and deceased are welcome in our home.

Helper

On January 29th of 2000, David went to work, clocked in and as he walked back to his truck and forklift repair shop at General Wax in North Hollywood, his boss, Scott, met him and they stopped and talked for awhile.

Scott said, "What's the matter, you aren't smiling today."

David replied, "I don't have nothing to smile about today...I'm through...today is my last day."

He had decided that he worked one century and that he would not work another. After work that day, he gathered up his tools and went home for the last time. That day was January 29th of 2000.

(If you have read our other books, by now you know David communicates with God's Angels and Entities, and refer to Joan Lee Harris' Angel as the Angel Jo or as the Angel Joleen.)

David had decided to start a website, but didn't know anything about making a website. For days, he studied and began building his website. But after a couple of months, he was getting discouraged as he sat at his computer and thought about quitting.

That day David thought, "What am I doing. I know nothing about building or running a website. Yes, I wanted to have a website that helps people in religion...people who were lost and didn't understand anything about God, but I'm old, and what do I do when bill collectors start knocking at my door?"

Then Jesus appeared and He said, "We have been here throughout your life. We were there when you had your heart attack and stood beside you as you had your by-pass, and we will stand beside you throughout your life. Don't worry about bill collectors; I will take care of them."

And then He was gone.

David recalls, throughout time Dan, our youngest son's life, he always talked about an Entity that called Himself the Helper. We never really thought much about it, but just knew that it was a good Angel that helped Dan throughout his life.

It was before Christmas in 1999, David believed, when a friend was in our home one evening as we, the friend, my oldest son, Tony, and David and I, sat in our dining room and talked.

Soon David said, "The Helper is here tonight."

Then David asked Dan to look for him.

Dan went from room to room, but could not find him. Then, Dan walked out into our garage, and when he returned he said, "The Helper is there in the garage."

David went into the garage and found Jesus standing at the rear door of our garage.

They talked for awhile and before He left, David said, "Thanks for coming."

He replied, "Anything for a brother."

And then He was gone.

Another night that David vividly remembered; after I went to sleep and he lay in bed, he asked the Angel Joleen, if She could help him remove the bad feelings about people that he would get.

She replied, "I cannot; only you can do that."

I then asked, "Can Jesus help me remove those feelings."

Immediately before She could answer, Jesus appeared with little lights flying all around Him, and He said, "Only you can remove those feelings, but I will help you."

He raised His hands and placed them on David and he felt His love flow through him as the little lights flew around Jesus and then they flew through David, too.

Then I woke up and saw Jesus. I started to cry. Jesus removed His hands from David and placed His hands on me, and I felt His love flow through me as I saw the little lights going into me. After a few minutes, They all left. I continued to cry and told David how I could not even speak the words to describe what I was feeling or what I had just experienced. I just said that it was a love that I had never in my whole life ever felt before. David just held me and we cried our tears of love together.

Another evening that David remembered was; as he sat and watched a program on television about Christianity, Jesus then appeared and said, "I did not ask to be worshipped, the Father is to be worshipped. They even have My birthday wrong; I was born on March 13th two years earlier."

In one conversation with the Angel Jo, She promised him that before he died She would ease his pains and would be there on the Other Side to hold and comfort him when he crosses over.

In a recent conversation David recalled, She stated, the night before he dies, David, our son Dan and I would see Her and She would tell us that the next day was the day for David to come Home once again. But the next day, he would forget because he would be helping people and not remember that was his day to come Home.

The Angel Jo, brings the deceased children through our home on their way to Heaven. And many times, we would find pizza left on the stove. David set video cameras up trying to record how the pizzas are cooked. The Angel Jo stated that some of the children wanted pizza before they move on, but then She laughs and added, "I don't know how they digest them."

And She stated that She cooks the pizzas in the wink of an eye so it wouldn't work trying to record it.

One day in the late1990s, when David was working at General Wax, he told another employee about Jonathon, a young boy killed in water in Florida, and that Dan and he had seen this child coming through our home on his way to Heaven. A few weeks later, the employee told him about a young relative of his that was killed by water in Florida, the murderer was the mother's boyfriend. In 2007, David went to Florida to visit the same fellow employee and friend from General Wax. The friend told David that today the mother of the deceased child continues to visit the child's grave every day. The murderer is now living in a Florida prison.

Over the past twelve years, we have noticed many children claiming that they have seen Jesus. I don't know if the children of today are more willing to talk about Jesus or not, but I do know that many children of today have not even heard of Him.

David and I have a very dear friend who happens to be a minister. At Christmas, he was putting up a Nativity Scene in his front yard. A little neighbor boy came and asked him what he was doing. Our friend told him he was building a Nativity Scene. The child asked him what a Nativity Scene was. My friend asked the little boy, "Do you not know the story of Christmas?"

The little boy replied, 'No" so our friend told him the story of Christmas. After the little boy left, our friend continued working on his Nativity Scene. Soon, another little boy came up to him and asked him what he was doing. Again, my friend explained what he was doing. By this time, our friend had Joseph, Mary and Jesus set up. He asked the little boy if he knew who they were. The little boy said as he pointed, "That's Jesus," as he pointed to Joseph, "That's the mom and that's the baby."

Our friend said, "No that's not Jesus. Do you know who they are? "Do you know the story of Christmas?"

Just as the other little boy, he replied, "No."

So once again, our friend told the little boy the story of Christmas. Our friend was just astounded that two little boys, from the same area, within a couple of hours of each other had come past his home and had never heard of the story of Christmas. Therefore, we don't know if more people today are seeing Him than ever before.

The Christian Bible states that when Jesus returns, all people will see Him. But it does not say if He will be in body or not. With more children seeing Him does that mean it is getting closer for all people to see Him?

We don't know.

Also we know it is said in the Muslim Religion that at the end of time, Jesus will appear and many people will ask Him to pray for them, and He will answer, "Why, you have many others to pray for you."

Prepare for Life

The Torah was accepted into the Christian Religion as the Old Testament and it was stolen into Islam as part of its rules. But the Muslims have merely stolen all that they claim came from Garbael to Muhammad. Nothing else needs to be said about that evil human Religion.

All three claim the story of Eden. And all say that man was Created before woman and God has placed His Wrath upon all females because of Eve deceiving Adam in the Garden.

The other female animals did nothing wrong. Their Scriptures say only the female, Eve, did sin, then why would a loving God punish all females?

If you go beyond the beliefs of man and turn to the Supreme Being, God, and Creation in the Universe, you would find that the fetus of an unborn child is female. And in the months after procreation, the unborn female child may become male. So actually the female is created before the male.

And if you believe in Scriptures about Adam and Eve, God kept His best Creation of human for last. Isn't that what God did with all of His other Creations? If God did indeed keep human for last, wouldn't He have kept His best Creation for last ...wasn't female His last Creation?

If you read all three of the bibles' Scriptures, you will find all three place female on the same level as male. (Men will not admit that women are his equal because man has turned his Religion toward himself and that places him above women.)

But in this reality that we live in, one partner needs to be the CEO and the other needs to be the CFO, and those two jobs of the family separates the male and female parents in a family.

David recalled, after he and I were married, that he told me that a marriage is like a business partnership that should grow stronger and richer in time, and if our love and marriage didn't become stronger and richer, than we should not be married.

Boy, did I ever get angry at him. But now, I understand that we are one; joined together and should make this a better place to live in as we prosper as a business in wealth and the knowledge of God.

An interesting fact that we once heard; if the three wise men were women, they would have brought formula, diapers and baby clothes and there would be peace on Earth.

During the early 2000s, David decided that it was time that we laid the past behind us and move forward in life. And it was in the fall of 2004, he rode his motorcycle from California to Ohio to a Haven family reunion. While he was there, he saw one of his older sisters and went over and sat with her so they could talk. She didn't have time for him, she kept returning to talk to their ex sister-in-law instead. Maybe she was ashamed that she had molested him when he was a child, or she just didn't want to see or talk with him, he left the reunion early.

In 2005, again he rode across to Ohio, this time, he went to see one of his brothers. As they sat in the brother's home and talked, their conversation turned to Hitler. David's brother's wife, who was from Germany, said, "In 1939, Hitler, told the Jews to leave... they should not have stayed." His brother agreed with her, and added, "That's right, they could have gotten out." Then, their conversation turned to the sexual abuse of the clergy, and his wife said, "They are only human." Again, his brother chimed in, "Yes, that's right."

David didn't say a word and left soon afterwards.

As David rode back across the U.S., he thought about what his brother said and when he arrived back at our home in California, he emailed his brother. David wrote him, "I can and do forgive you for your sexual molestation against me when I was a child, but I cannot forgive you for saying Hitler was right in killing all those people, and the clergy were right for doing those things against God's Children."

He never heard from him again. Why?

Was it because David did not agree with him about Hitler and the clergy, or was it because of what he did to David when he was a child?

When it comes down to it, it really is not David's concern. It is between him and God.

If people that are around you do things that you feel is wrong, get away from them, and if they later change in life, that is not your concern. A true friend will not do anything that is against his friend. Stand fast on your beliefs if you truly feel that you are following your heart and that is what God wants us to do.

If you have done things that you now feel or know was wrong, don't do them again.

We as humans, will do things that may be considered wrong. When you find your mistake, repent, change your views of the past, and do not make the same mistake twice.

Yes, it is true that we will live as long as we have a descendant living through that descendants DNA. The human laws cannot change our DNA, only nature can, but our likes or dislikes are left up to the individual. This reality is a place that we do not have to make the same mistakes that our ancestors did.

In the 1800s, prisons were designed to separate prisoners but this lead to inmates becoming insane because the human animal cannot live without inner acting with other humans. And the inner reacting, connections with other family members, helps in the sanity of the individual human. In the mid 70s, we were taught to send our children to their rooms for "time out" whenever we could not control them. The isolation of our children has caused them to become independent on their concepts when dealing with other humans, thus our children cannot have a lasting relationship with the opposite sex, and today more are turning toward homosexuality instead of heterosexuality because they cannot deal with the opposite sex.

God does not make mistakes, humans do, and everything is planned into His Master Plan of life. There is no gender in His Angels. Gender of DNA comes from the things that are designed upon our Deoxyribonucleic Acid from our ancestors. And those traits may have come from either the males or females from our past. Our disabilities or imperfections may have come from the selections of the partners of our ancestors, but that too was known as part of God's Master Plan.

The problem of homosexuality comes from our inability to relate to the opposite sex that first started from isolation, learning, in childhood. But, a late Christian friend once said, "Today, there are too many in the world, maybe it would be better if there were more Homos."

Islam is the only Religion that remains that brain-washes its young into beliefs of their god, and that, too, is taught by man to include all that is desired by Muslim men. Most Muslims are homosexuals or inverts molesting their own daughters, but if they do not "use" the vaginal, it is merely a sex act, and the female remains a virgin and worth more money when they sell her.

But let's move on, the human body is replacing cells every minute throughout our lives, and if a few of the cells are produced abnormal and the body does not destroy them, then the body will begin to produce more of the abnormal cell. The human body is designed to contain over 700 cancer cells at any given moment. Cigarette smoking does not cause cancer, but it helps the cancer cells to multiply. The growth of cancer cells is caused by the human replication system and not by tobacco smoking. Nicotine may cause cells to be produced abnormally. All of the chemicals that we put on and in our bodies are causing cancer. We are living in a world of people that do not like the smell of burning tobacco and are out-lawing the smoking of tobacco. They cannot realize that automobiles, alcohol and other drugs are harming the human bodies worse, but the true problem is; people enjoy those things more than smelling burning tobacco.

Throughout California and probably in every state across the U.S., gasoline filling stations have placed warning signs on their pumps that says, "Gasoline contains known substance that causes Cancer."

Do people read and understand that the gas that they are putting into their cars is more dangerous smoking cigarettes today?

Less people smoke today than the gasoline we burn in our cars!

Do people realize that putting Marijuana or Pot into their bodies, as breathing anything that is in the air, into their lungs in destorying their lungs?

Gasoline put about 90% of its matter (pollutions) into the air, a cigarette put only about 15% of its matter into the air.

What is more?

A gallon of gasoline or a mere cigarette.

Do the people realize everything that put on their bodies are killing cells in their bodies?

Do the people know that being fat is causing their body to produce more cells and some of those cells are cancerous?

We are living in a world in which we cannot change the concepts of other people. Let others do what they wish. This life is a place where we should get straight with God, and no other person besides you can do that for you because all of life is individual.

Experience all that everyone will share with you. If they are liars, or do things that you do not agree with, forget them and go on your way, for it is not your concern what others think or do. So do what is right for you and not other people.

Enjoy life and experience it; look around and see all the things that God has created for you to enjoy and be happy that you had time to live in this day. When you wake up in the morning to that beautiful sunrise and hear the birds singing their songs as they perch in the green tree tops, or when you watch the sun set in its glowing red ambers in the quiet of the evening as the day comes to an end, remember that God, the Creator, put those things here for us to experience and enjoy. Keep in mind that even the bad that occurred in your life was meant for you to experience because all things were part of God's Master Plan.

Do you remember the old saying, "Living better through chemicals"?

This remains the concept of today.

The Length of Life

Every life has a length that the individual will endure in his life time.

David tells the story; his Great-Grandfather, Francis Marion Haven, was born on June 14, 1844, and died on March 27, 1908, in his home near Flint Springs, Kentucky. He was a Hero for the Union in the Civil War.

David's dad, Estil J. Haven, was born January 11, 1901, in Flint Springs, Kentucky, and moved his family to Wooster, Ohio, in the 1920s.

(David's dad past on in 1989.)

It took David's parents three days to make the trip when they moved to Wooster, Ohio from the Beaver Dam area of Kentucky. Today, that same trip takes around 8 hours.

The other day, David and I were talking about life, and he said, "Do you realize that we have lived in this house for 10 years?

"And did you know that the Angel Jo re-entered back into my life and into your life in the fall of 1996…just 12 years ago."

After much conversation about the length of life, I added, "I just realized that I am old. I was 39 when Jo entered into my life. Tony will be 39 in just eight more years. I am going to be 52 years old this fall. It just hit me that I am in my fifties and Buddy, my oldest brother, just bought a house last year. He will be 60 this fall. And my oldest sister is still renting and her husband is nearly 58 now. Where did the time go?"

We view our pet's life as short and know the little dogs may live between 14 to 18 years. That's nothing!

Our lives are nothing, too, when we think about life being a mere 60 to 80 years, if we are lucky. No one is here forever, each will die when his time is up.

Many times, David has told me, that he would love to live with me for another 1,000 years, but he doesn't want to be old. Everything changes around us daily, and David said, "I don't want to see the differences that are coming to the world, and I thank God for the 'clock of life' that I contain."

Everyone is in the exact place in time that we are supposed to be, God does not make mistakes.

Enjoy life and do not allow others to place their demands upon you.

Remember, everyone is alive today, and everyone will die someday.

There is no need to cry when someone dies. Did you think that they would live forever?

Be happy for the life that they lived on this earth and the experiences which they endured while here.

If life was continual, the child could never be the parent. The parent would continue to tell their children what to do. Do you wish to live as the child forever?

Death is allowing the child to grow into adulthood and closer to God before the child's life is over. Allow your children the experiences that you enjoyed. But their experiences could and should be enjoyed before your demise.

Do not place demands on any of your children when they become adults just as your ancestors did not place demands on to you.

There are three steps in life; birth, life and death, and each person will experience each step of life. There is no exceptions.

Life is not a dress rehearsal, once It's over It's over. You will not be back again. And like David said before, "Life is short when compared to Eternity."

Death

Every living thing has a built-in clock that says how long that body will last. Presently, humans do not possess the intelligence to read and understand all that includes the built-in time clock program that is instilled into our DNA. And if the living thing is left alone without others contributing or assisting to that life, it would remain as long as it was procreated into that person's DNA clock.

David used to tell the doctors the differences between them and him was; he was a mechanic, and if he, a mechanic, cannot fix the problem with a vehicle, the owner would bring it back again and again until it's fixed while doctors bury their mistakes.

At graduation, a doctor receives a license to merely practice medicine, we live in a world where mechanics do not practice their jobs. Doctors are pretty good in setting broken bones but that is about all, we are still very primitive in medicine.

David never could understand why children are not taught about death because they will see many people die within their lifetimes.

My mother had recently passed away. I missed her dearly. One afternoon, I was talking with my older sister, Kathy, who had just taken her young granddaughter, McKenzie, home.

Kathy told me that when she was going to take her granddaughter home, she had asked Kathy to take her to see her Uncle Bud first.

Kathy asked her why and she said, "Well, when Grandma died, Uncle Bud said that she was going to be down in that big hole in the ground for a long time and I think she has been down there long enough and we should go get her and bring her home."

This brought tears to my eyes.

Kathy explained to McKenzie that only Grandma's body was in the ground and that Grandma was actually up in Heaven with God.

McKenzie looked up into the sky and said that that was an awful long way to go.

Most churches do teach children that people that are deceased are in Heaven with God. Why do we not teach our children about death?

Is it because we do not really understand it ourselves?

(David always understood that when we die, life would continue as it does here today; he would be living in a world where he would go home to his parents house, and visit with them, and he would go to the store and back to his home and life would continue on as it does here on earth.)

The concept of reincarnation was thought to be the rebirth of the Soul in successive bodies. But reincarnation is a myth designed by humans to help explain what death is and to help ease the thoughts of death from humans.

(The Angel-within, that part of God that dwells within you, could have lived others lives before you, but they are not your lives. And they may share some of its earlier lives' stories with you, and those life stories you may have considered as reincarnation.)

Everyone should realize or be taught that death is the 3rd part of life that we all will experience someday. God did not promise anyone a lifetime that would out-live friends and family. Is that what you wanted; to see all of your friends and family die before you.

Whatever the reason for death, be it by nature or others, all people will die someday. The Soul does not leave the body, the body leaves the Soul as it, the body, goes back to that of which it came – the dirt.

The Soul is the recorded experiences of that life of the deceased human only. And the Soul is the only part of life that should live with God.

David and I had a friend that worked for the City of Los Angeles. One day he went to work but decided to come back home before his workday started. He just wanted to tell his wife and kids that he loved them. Later that same day he died in a tragic on the job accident.

On Easter Morning in 1989, my father wanted to visit with some friends. After he visited with friends, my mother walked into the house and found him lying dead on the floor from a heart attack.

Many people have reported that whenever a relative is dying and is near death, that person will be visited by those who have past on earlier. They tell of conversations that those close to death have had with the deceased. This also happened with David's oldest brother, Jim, who was visited by his deceased wife before his death.

It seems those who are near death and those who may feel they are near dying could be more in tuned to the Other Side than before.

And many people tell of taking photos in their homes that contain the deceaseds Entities in those photos. A few photo studios have told us that they have seen many photos containing Entities like the photo of Joan Lee Harris, that we have hanging on our living room wall.

Whenever an organ stops working in the body, all other organs begin to send out signals requesting help to the brain because they are in trouble and are dying. The organs - the body, wants to live and demands help via the central nervous system to the brain. These signals ring out through the body and continue for a few minutes after the body ceases; these cries sound out after life ends and as the Soul - the recorded experiences, leaves the body, it begins its travel to the Other Side with the Angel-within.

The human had a lifetime to accept the Creator into his life.

(Accepting the Creator into one's life; allowing part of God, one of His Angels, to experience the life that the human lived, as living the time that experiences occurs. Our life experiences are what separate humans from all other living things on earth. And that is the part of life, God's Gift of Life, that is part of God, His Angel, dwells within the human for experiencing our decision of actions and reactions. Accepting the Creator into one's life does not mean becoming religious, it means to accept the nature of life, allowing Him to live your life along side of Him. Our bodies are the vessel that we share with an Angel of God, if we desire that to be. If we do not allow His Angel entry, than we are no-thing to God just as all other living things are to God.)

After the death of a person, the deceased body looses about 2 ounces. And as the Soul leaves the body, the Soul's screams may be heard. The screams last into the Other Side as the Soul ascends toward God.

Our two sons and David hear the screams of the deceased that just cross over. All death is painful. The Angel Jo has told David that She will ease his pains here on earth before his death and She will hold and comfort him when he crosses over.

Life is for experiencing your actions and reactions. But when life is over, the experiencing ends, there is no more to continue as experiencing. When life ends, your life will end also. You past life should be with God. Your past life; all that you have endured through the years of your life. This is the part of you that should live forever with God.

We will not live in Heaven where life will continue as here on Earth. We will not live day by day experiencing actions as we do here on Earth. All continuation will cease after life. Our life's stories were created for God and His Angels to experience what we felt about our thoughts of our actions and reactions. And when we die, we will not continue to inner-act with others again.

God's individual Angels will be able to step back in to your life and see (live) what you felt during that time. The Angel will be able to feel how you loved another, and also be able to feel how that person loved you. The Angel will be able to walk back into time (past) and see what and how the actions from you and others affected people, but They cannot change that past. But They may assist (inspire) you in changing the future. The past is chiseled into stone, repent and change your views for the future. You will not live forever, but your past life experiences (all that you did and all that you do) will live forever with God.

If you do not allow God to be a part of your life, His Angels will not be able to re-live your past or assist you in changing your future because then you will be no-thing to Him.

God never said that we would spend eternity down on our knees worshipping Him… man said that.

If God wanted us to be His slaves, He wouldn't have needed us to go through life before.

Jesus never said that He was God… Man said that.

After the death of Jesus, Christians were hunted as other cult members by Roman Soldiers. Christians Services moved into the houses where the woman led the services. It was at this time Heaven was seen as a large banquet where they had plenty of food to eat.

(This belief of Heaven was plenty of food came from the people on Earth at that time were starving.)

Once humans learn that religion brought in money, Christianity was made into big business. Then the services that were lead by women was removed to allow man to be in control of God, and that made the story of Adam and Eve believable.

It was during the following years of Christianity, one had to pay the church in order for them or their deceased loved-one to go to Heaven.

When the church income became smaller, the church realized that the people didn't have enough money to pay, and the idea of praying the deceased into Heaven came next. But still, the ideas of Heaven, where a person wanted to remain forever; with streets paved with gold and everyone living in mansions first evolved.

The churches made people believe that life continues on the Other Side with God in Heaven.

The idiotic religion of Islam says; one must submit to Allah by his age of around 43, and if one that dies and goes to Hell will only stay in Hell for 7 years, and all who is a believer in Allah will someday be in Heaven with Muhammad. But to be a believer in Allah, one must first be a Muslim. What other religion tells its people that all who believe in their god will get to Heaven in time?

Jesus and His life didn't even fit into the concepts of the Jewish Messiah.

Jesus' followers defined His life into a Religion. And God does know the future because He knew Jesus' death was needed for Christianity to be born.

Everything that the Jews and Romans did to Jesus was part of the known Master Plan of God's. He knows everything that you will do, we only live for our feelings of our actions.

A friend once said, "If everything is known in God's Master Plan, then why should I do anything?"

David answered, "If you do nothing, then God's Master Plan contained you not doing anything. Do what ever you feel like doing because that, too, is known in His Master Plan."

The Other Side

Many people have reported dying in hospitals, during operations, or in automobile accidents that came back to life afterwards. Many of those people claimed going to the Other Side and seeing a light. And some will talk or write about seeing Jesus or others, that help them return to life again.

A few years ago, a friend told David about her two personal experiences she had with the Other Side and the Light.

In the first one, she tried to commit suicide when she was young.

On the Other Side, she was in a dark place, standing on a bridge. On the far side of the bridge stood her family members that had previously past over. They kept telling her to go back because it was not time for her. Some people on this side of the bridge told her to come back. Of course, she came back to this side and to life.

Her second encounter with the Light was; she had surgery and died for a few minutes on the operating table.

This time she was in the Light. She said the place was beautiful. She heard some kind of music. It was a different kind of music than she had ever heard before.

And someone asked her if she wanted to return to earth or not, and then they showed her the future. She saw her son and daughter as they are now with good lives. They told her she needed to come back and help others. She decided to return and did.

Waking up in a hospital bed, a nurse told her everything would be all right and left the room. Later, she tried to find that nurse. The hospital staff said there was no nurse that worked there with the name she had been given. Who was that nurse… an Angel?

David guessed, you could say that he first started observing and studying Entities around 61 years ago, when he was about two years old. When he was younger, he always said that he did not want them to leave because he was learning about their world.

The Angel Jo first entered into David's life in the fall of 1996, and she introduced him to Gabrael, and then Michael, and then all three introduced him to Jesus. And from that time, he studied under all four of the Angels, 24 hours a day and 7 days a week. Therefore, you should know that he knows what he is talking about when it comes to Entities, Angels and the Other Side.

(David has seen Entities and Angels with Hell and Heaven in their hearts and has seen many who are lost on the Other Side. We will get into the different locations where they remain in the coming Chapters of this book. And maybe what David has learned will help you understand what life is.)

You created your Heaven or Hell from what you did in life here on Earth.

Life is a Gift from God. But yes, He did know everything that would happen in your life because all life is part of His Master Plan.

We should not judge people, but we should judge their actions to see if they are acceptable for us as humans to do.

We should not do anything bad or evil and blame God because what we did was known in His Master Plan. If we change the direction of our lives, then that change was known in His Master Plan, too. We are completely responsible for our actions and re-actions. We are the ones who decide what is right or wrong for us, God has shown us the differences between good and bad, we decide what is correct for us. We as all humans created the actions of our Hells.

Once life is over and your Soul is connected to an Angel. That means the Angel is connected to your Energy that you contained when alive!

The Energy is your Soul that your recorded life experiences are placed upon.

That Angel is part of the congregation that makes up God. If the Angel does not like the life that you lived, He will not want other Angels to see or feel as you did in life. These Angels (Entities) run-away on the Other Side because they do not want others to know them. Sometimes, they do not think their lives were bad, and they will try to go into God's Heaven. But once they walk into the Light and understand life, they will leave because it was you that lead their lives, you had the decision to be good or bad; it was you that had the bad thoughts and did thing against the people. To live in this world, your body must have solid matter. After removing the solid matter (death), your Soul remains.

The Soul is the Energy that your life's experiences are recorded upon. Once the human dies, the Soul is attached to an Entity (Angels) as the Soul leaves the body and enters into the Other Side. The Soul is what the Angel carries to the congregation of Angels that make up God.

If the Angel-within has experienced a good life, then that Angel is covered with the Light of God – good feelings, and will see and will be able to go to the Light. But if the Angel-within, has experienced an evil, bad life, that Angel is covered with veils of self-centered pleasures. And the Angel-within, could contain different life experiences from different lives, depending on if the Angel had other lives.

Many times the human's life story (Soul), the things that the individual did may be too much for the Angel-within to bear. And when this occurs the Angel may not be able to support the life style of the human, those things will contaminate the Angel, and the Angel will not allow itself to come in to contact with others, and will run away into the darkness on the Other Side.

You cannot examine a single strand of life to know the life's complete picture, you must examine the complete ball of string to understand the life, and that is the reason why we should not judge others.

All people have the ability to leave their bodies and travel to distant places and the Other Side, but the problem is most people refuse this Gift from God, or have been taught that it is evil to do what is not written into their religion.

David learned as a young child how to leave his body and travel with the Angels or without the Angels, on the Other Side. He guessed traveling to places on Earth did not concern him back then.

During the last half of the 1990s, traveling with the Angels became a nightly event before he went to sleep, and God's Angels taught him many things as their traveled during those nights.

He has traveled on the Other Side, and he has seen his Angel-within, Jacob, many times. He was covered with what looked like sores and lesions. With time he was able to heal Him and remove His Hells that he, or His other lives had made for Him.

As a true Father, God does not place demands upon His children. He would never demand that you must be down upon your knees praying to Him or anyone else forever, humans do that. There was no need for us to go through this life, if God wanted us to be His slaves.

Contrary to religious beliefs there is <u>no</u> rank in God or in Heaven. Man has placed rank in God and Heaven to control the people. And we can observe man's comtemptment toward God in this place, the world, where men still have slaves.

God does not need us to fight Holy Wars for Him, humans do that. He created everything and that includes evil, all is His. Do you really think He would not fight Himself?

God does not need 10% of your earnings or tidings, but humans do. Again, He created everything, even the money. He doesn't need us to give Him anything. But if the churches charged for entrance, it would be a profit organization and would be charged more taxes from our governments, but as a non-profit organization, it has lower taxes. And all churches can and most do have some type of board that rules and receives most of the money as their pay from the church.

In the stories of Scriptures, God and His Son, Jesus, did intervene in the lives of humans, and would do so now if that was needed. His Angels, part of Him, is with us daily in our lives. Presently, the only time that corrupted humans need God is when they die. And at death, the human will cry out, "Oh, my God," or, "God, please help me."

Entities that have only lived as children seem to have the most difficult, but also women that were mothers need help in going to God's Heaven, too. But there are many Angels of God's that help those find their way to God, but children and women seem to have the hardest time leaving behind the living. Many come through our home, and they call me the Guider, as I help the Angel Joleen and Jesus deliver them to the Light. The Other Side has no location. It is neither up or down, it's not to the left or right, and it is not a place of the past or future because it's all of these things and places at this time.

All locations are present on the Other Side. Others that came before you may be there with you at this time on the Other Side. And this is the place where you will judge yourself and decide if your Soul will remain with God in Heaven or Hell, or just on the Other Side, or if you were No-thing to God. And at death, this will be your Judgment Day.

The Light

The Light is the accumulated life experiences of all Angels – God. This knowledge of God is experienced as being bright as a the Light, a wonderful place in Heaven.

When in the Light, you will have all the knowledge that God possesses, when you leave the Light, you will only remember your life experiences.

The Angel Jo, has told David, "Gabrael comes from the Light and tells me things that I am to tell you. I've been away too long."

David and Jo have been to many places on the Other Side as well as places on this side.

One place that they have been is a long wall that they regularly played on or near. David has often asked Her, "What is on the Other Side?"

She always answered, "I don't know, we have not been there."

On the Other Side, they contain the thoughts of today's life, and not the knowledge that the Light contains.

Many books and a few movies have been written about Near Death Experiences, NDEs.

The people that experienced NDEs need not have died or stayed dead to experience this event. Many times, the individual may have been sleeping or subconscious during those happenings. But we hear about NDEs whenever the person dies and then returns to live. But many people experience NDEs than we realize, and others could experience NDEs if they would allow themselves the pleasure.

The NDEs seem to follow the individual's personality and/or the characteristics of the individual. Whereas, some have seen deceased family members or friends, in a Heaven type of setting while others may have seen a place with a resemblance of Hell.

One story, it makes David laugh, is of a woman who claims to have seen a Heaven with a board of twelve men who ruled. There is no rank in Heaven or God, only man conceived rank here on Earth!

Many will see where their lives have led to; they may see Heaven or Hell as they are living.

We see what we want to perceive as our Eternity, be it good or bad. But God may be giving those individuals the opportunity to change the direction of their lives. And this may be where they are going if they do not change the direction of their life.

The Light is the congregation of Angels that make up God. The deceased are drawn toward Him, that is what the Souls see - God as the Light of His knowledge.

Once life is over, it's gone…it's as if chiseled in stone. You cannot go back and change it. You have up to the end of your life to change whatever you did. But you should not wait until your life is nearly over to be nice to others.

The old "Born again" Christians also make David laugh, too. They cannot wait until their lives are near its end and expect to be saved. We see them going into restaurants daily to have their little luncheons, carrying their little Bibles that proudly proclaims they are saved. During their luncheons and afterwards, they always demonstrate the style of life that they lived. And their actions indicate that they have not changed their life styles. Their actions of Salvation will not come when they know what is coming – death. They cannot go back in time and change their past that they knew was wrong.

Those as the children, who do not know of God are most rewarded in Heaven, and not the grown-ups who did badly and then confess without changing the directions of their past.

Repent while you have time, change your views of the past and find your individual Salvation for the future. The people will not look down upon you for changing your views of life. Life is so short, does it matter to others if you now believe in God or the afterlife?

Your life is not my concern; my only concern is my life.

If you change your views of the past, you will still be the strong man that you were yesterday, but a stronger man with God in your heart.

Remember all others will endure death sometime during their life, and once their life is over, they will not be back and you will not be able to ask them for forgiveness, nor can they ask you for forgiveness. Once again, life is not a dress rehearsal.

Directions to Hell

And the Angel Jo said unto David, "The Directions to Hell are the negative actions of humans that are from self-centerness feelings, that drives a wedge between you - your Soul and the Congregation of God."

There are many roads to Hell and others are willing to give you directions, but no one knows where the road will lead you.

The individual's concepts may direct others to their Hells. A prime example of this is the English language.

Back in the 60's, a separation of generations occurred. We no longer understood our children and their language. What caused this to happen?

Why did the same words we had always used, as well as our parents, all of a sudden take on a whole new meaning to our children?

For example, let's take the word "gay". When we were children, we would say we were happy and gay, meaning we were happy and carefree. Today if you use the word gay, it is associated with homosexuality.

People before the 60's knew the meaning of words. If we were to ask our parents what a word meant, they would tell us and more than likely they would get the dictionary out so we could also read the meaning of the word. We were taught by our parents.

For some reason in the 60's we stopped talking to our children. We didn't seem to have time for them. Our children started making up their own meaning of words. Another example of this is the word hazing. Today our children think this means things you need to do for your job. They think it means respect. However, if you go to the dictionary you will find it means "to subject newcomers or initiates to pranks or humiliating horseplay".

David has also found, not only with our own children but with children of friends and family, that if you try to correct a child on a definition of a word, they get angry. Are they really angry with you?

No!

They get angry with themselves for not knowing the meaning of the word. But who is really to blame for their anger?

It is us, the parents. If only we would have taken the time to talk to them, but we didn't. They would listen to a word being used in a sentence and come up with their own meaning of the word. Our children were taught by themselves and their peers. This action puts us in Hell.

Can we fix this language problem?

Will we fix this language problem or is it too late?

Only we as individuals can learn from these actions and only God and his Master Plan knows the answer to that. But remember that ALL things are possible with God.

As human, we may think of our bad doings, actions, as "getting even" with others.

In God's Creation, the individual human controls his Hells and Heaven, and that person's individual place of Eternity comes from all that the person did in life. And many times, it may seem as though the experiences do not come from bad actions that were done to another, but God does not make mistakes; He allows us to do what is needed for us and that designates Eternity for us as individuals.

The concept of "Karma" does not mean its re-actions must occur now, instead its actions may come after the death of that person. And that statement of "Karma" stays in the concept of "God Moves in Mysterious Ways;"

His actions against the evil act may not come until the end of time.

And the statement, "Go with the Flow" means, do not allow things that get you down to be the actions that get you to return to others.

"Go with the Flow", means allow others to do what they wish, and do not turn the other cheek so they can strike it; guard yourself and protect the Angel within.

Another statement is, "Peace of mind is worth the truth."

And that statement is how most people of the world live today; in Hell. It should be noted, that "Peace of mind is not worth the truth" when it involves others. When this phrase occurs, people are lazy. This happens when that statement places yourself in domination of others, and that is a Sin.

Allowing others to make statements that you do not fully believe in, is not worth the truth, and that allows them to place you into their domination because it allows others to judge for you. And allowing others to do your thinking is self-domination.

All actions, even the good and bad, have repercussions. The statement, 'We Reap what we Sow" and "We get our just Rewards" mean the same thing. And all of our actions become permanent in the end, after life.

One true indication of a person that is in Hell is the way people act at Funerals; usually those who cry the hardest are the ones who treated the deceased badly or the deceased treated those mourners badly. The deceased or the living, cannot go back in time and control the deceased, or the deceased cannot control their lives anymore.

But we should not judge others, we should re-view their actions to see if they are correct for us. By judging the actions of the mourners, we are judging their actions to see if that is the way we should treat the living, you cannot go back in time and change the deceased's life.

At the same time, keep in mind that when the time comes and your life as well as your spouses life has been completed on this earth, the two of you shall stand together before God. Therefore, if you have lived a good life and kept God in your heart, loved all others and placed no domination on anyone, but your spouse did not adhere to God's words and did evil things in his/her life and you knew about it and stood beside them, then you shall be judged as doing the same. By standing beside your spouse, you allowed yourself to be placed into self-domination by your spouse.

However, if you kept God in your heart, loved all others and placed no domination on anyone, but your spouse deceived you by allowing you to believe that he/she was following the same path you were following, but was actually doing evil deeds, then you shall not be held responsible for his/her actions.

To help you understand domination and self-domination, I have a scenario that should help you understand; walk into a room that contains a table and on that table lays a pair of sunglasses. Now stand near the table and place your feet firmly on the floor, and try to pick up the sunglasses. Did you pick the sunglasses up?

The scenario said, Try to pick up the sunglasses, it did not say, to pick up the sunglasses. People will only retain about 15% of what they read, hear and understand, and only 15% of what is said, but think they know the complete story of what others meant because all people think they know everything. Hence, what is right is right and what is wrong is nobody.

Life is easier for people if they let others think for them. And what most think will place your concepts in Hell.

To further understand what causes Hell, David has been closely watching the events unfold in Israel, and this has caused him to study the Islamic Religion.

The following are good examples of the Sin of following others, self-dominations. These true stories explain how people are drawn into conditions of life styles that will place them in Hell after life.

The Islamic Religion speaks of one Muslim nation with no borders nor boundaries. That indicates, if there are no boundaries or borders to their nation, they are speaking of one nation that covers the world.

(And this is what's happening to our southern border with Mexico. The way to repair our southern border dilemma is to make Mexico into a state of the U.S.A.)

And yet, today the Muslim countries have different leaders. But, they speak of a nation that has no man-made laws. Can you imagine a country with no man-made laws... where no one is in charge?

Everyone does as he wishes.... no one needs to work, if you need money, just take it from someone who has money. The stores would be open only the hours that its owner wishes. And if you wanted to have a store, just kill a store owner and take it, no laws would stop you. And if you kill another, just pay off his family and you will not need to go to jail. Neither God nor Allah wrote the words for Islam, man wrote Islamic bible, so whose laws do Muslims follow?

Equal rights for all the people of the Islamic Religion... there is none. They believe that Muhammad will be born to man, and women will be the beast of burden once again. Also, they state, "No formal education or medical care for women."

(Even today, Muslim men buy and sell women of any age.)

The Palestinians speak of their suicide bombers as martyrs, a martyr as one who dies, suffers or gives up everything for his religion - Allah. The understanding of the word "Martyr" is one who is persecuted. The Israelis are being persecuted, not the Palestinians. Palestinians are not dying for their religion; they are dying for control over Israel and for control over the people of the world. The Islamic religion is racist, and Yasser Arafat is a racist and pushing policies for ethnic cleansing of the Israelis.

The present Palestinian uprising started because the Prime Minister of Israel, Ariel Sharon, visited a Holy site. The Palestinians cast the first stone, the Israelis reacted in self-defense. And the Israelis retaliated only to the ugly acts of gorilla warfare from the cowardly Palestinian leaders, who told their people that if they die fighting the Israelis, they will go to Heaven.

(Their Heaven is a sexual heaven where they will find 72 virgins waiting for them. Is that Heaven for the virgins?)

While the Palestinian officials cry out that they are sending in suicide bombers and killing the Israelis because the Israelis killed Muslims first. The Palestinians were the first to kill Israelis at the start of this uprising, but does it matter who died first?

This is not a Holy War or a war for freedom; this is a war by man for ownership of land and a power trip of a few Muslims.

Muhammad was given God's words, but his followers and the Palestinians have turned those words into words of the dog. After Muhammad died, his followers demanded others to join their religion, and if they refused, they were put to death. Even today, those who convert to Christianity from the Islamic religion are put to death, if found out.

All the people of the world need to rally behind the Israelis now, because the Palestinians will not stop their fighting until they have control over Israel, and if they do defeat Israel, someday soon we, too, will be fighting the Muslims in our home lands, for the fall of the Israeli people will be the beginning to the end of the civilized world. And this is occurring because of people thinking, "Peace of Mind is Worth the Truth." We live in a world where the people believe there is peace if they are not fighting in their home land.

Yes, David and I believe as told to him by the Angels, "Taking of a life is not the answer." But They, the Angels, did not say that the corrupt Islam should not be erased from the world.

But if the Israelis cannot Inspire the Palestinians to live in peace, then the Palestinians must be dealt with as needed, because we cannot let a group of people that do or do not call themselves a nation, and who are backed by terrorist, dictate to any other group of people. We cannot allow the Israelis to become enslaved as they were during World War Two under the dictation of Hitler.

May the one God who is above Muhammad, Jesus and Moses, who is the God that Abraham, Isaac and Jacob worshipped, have mercy on the Palestinian's and the Muslim's Souls.

Late one night last week as David stood in our back yard garden, the Angel Jo said to him, "Domination directed from others toward you, you cannot stop. But you can stop their domination from causing you self-domination. Do not live in Hell because of what others think or do.

"If you plant a tree in your front yard and another says he does not like that tree and states he will rip it out when you are asleep, he has placed his domination over you because you cannot stop what others think or say. But know what you do concerning that tree is controlled by the domination. For if you stand guard on that tree, then, his domination has placed you in self-domination of guarding that tree, because you would not have needed to guard that tree if he had not said that. And if you remove that tree, then, his words of not liking the tree has caused you to remove it, thus, his domination has then placed self-domination over you. Or if you construct a fence around the tree to protect it, he has caused you to build a fence, thus again; he has placed his domination over you. Or, if your 'dog' wishes, you could kill him, but that too, caused you to do something that you did not wish to do, and that action would control the rest of your life as you lived in prison for murder."

Then Jesus said to David, "When someone slaps you, turn the other cheek. That does not mean to stand there and allow them to slap your other cheek. It means to forget what they have done and hold no remorse against them for if you do, then they have placed you in self-domination. Thus, taking of another's life is not the answer. But yet, you must protect yourself from the aggression of others. And do not become a slave.

"Once many years ago as I stood at the edge of a cliff, the Satan said to Me, 'Your Father will save you, jump.' I replied to him, 'I will not tempt God.' The word 'tempt' that I used meant, 'coax' or 'demand.' If I would have jumped, I would have been demanding the Father to save Me.

"But there is no Satan or Devil, there is only man's desire to control others. Satan and the Devil were created by man for control over others.

"God's Will is written into every story of the Christian Bible, 'To love all people and have no domination toward them,' and My life was a living demonstration on how people are to live as God wills. It does not take a college graduate to understand life, for the ones who have not heard or have not seen are the most rewarded in Heaven. And yet, God - the Father, does not dominate, so why does the human try to dominate?

"The human only tried to dominate whenever he allows the dog to control his life. You must follow the Angel-within to live a righteous life, for then, it does not matter if you have seen or heard for you shall be the most rewarded in Heaven.

"Whenever one tries to place domination over you, they do not seek God – the Supreme One, therefore, do not listen to them. If they were seeking God - following their Angel-within, they would have never tried to place domination over you.

"If someone tries to place demands on you, do as the Angel Jo and We do, stand fast and say nothing, but do not allow them to place you in self-domination, therefore, do not tempt the Angel-within who is part of God.

"Those who have learned how to hate from the dogs cannot be inspired unless they wish it. Hatred comes from evil and cannot be viewed as Love. Whenever you hear a 'preacher' talk of things he hates, he is speaking from the dog. God has created everything, even the evil, but He does not hate the bad; He dislikes the evil. And yet, the evil was needed for individual choices to experience. You were taught by the dogs, and later, you were inspired to know God. People can change; you are living proof that demonstrates this. Others can change if they desire change.

"The people of the world need to be inspired to know that they own nothing. They did not create it, the Creator owns all that He created. The people just have guardianship of that item until their end. As a gold prospector, you do not own the gold that you dig out of the ground; you merely own the labor - that part of time of your life that it took you to dig the gold out of the earth. The automobile that you have is not yours. You do not own the material that went into it, God owns that. He created all the materials on earth. You only bought the labor that went into making the car. You paid someone for the labor that it took to make the car. You traded money for his labor - part of his life.

"The Israelis and Palestinians fight over land that neither own, God owns it. Yasser Arafat became chairman of the PLO in 1969, and when the Palestinians had their own country, the PLO was started to overtake Israel. The Muslims speak of 'Holy Wars,' God does not need mere mortals to fight His wars, if He had wars to fight, but remember, He created everything, do you think He would have created anything that He needed to fight?

"Yasser Arafat is the founder of terrorism that is known today. Osama bin Laden is just one who learned evil ways from Arafat, how to use terrorism for his own gain. And those who fight under the thoughts of 'Holy Wars' are fools and cannot be inspired to seek God. I cannot and will not tell you what to do with these types of people; the answer must come from you - the Angel-within. If I told you what should be done, then, I would be dominating you, and your actions are your individual choices of life. And if you follow what is in your heart, you shall be seeking God, and His Will shall be done."

David then asked the Angels to tell him more about Islam, and Gabrael appeared and said to him, "I was the one who they claimed talked with Muhammad in the desert. But it did not matter if God, I or the evil Energy that you call Satan or the Devil communicated with him, for Muhammad polluted the conversation with his thoughts and ideas, for he was inspired 180 degrees from what it is said, I have told him. Then later, his followers corrupted his religion with their thoughts and ideas.

"God does not disapprove of Islam, for He allowed it to be created. Therefore, He dislikes it, but man created it for control of men.

Hatred comes from evil, dislike comes from love and the Father - the Creator. You may make something and dislike it, but you will not disapprove of it or you would have never made it or maybe, you would have destroyed it. God disapproves of terrorist, for terrorism comes from individual evil choices. God does not make mistakes, humans do."

(For those who do not understand what the war in Israel is and the war on terrorist is about, the following will help you comprehend the terrorist - Palestinian thinking, and all Muslins think the same.)

Below is the Palestinian National Covenant, the official charter of the Palestine Liberation Organization (PLO). The text is the English version published officially by the PLO, unabridged and unedited.

Note, however, that the PLO's translation sometimes deviates from the original Arabic so as to be more palatable to Western readers. For example, in Article 15, the Arabic is translated as "the elimination of Zionism," whereas the correct translation is "the liquidation of the Zionist presence." "The Zionist presence" is a common Arabic euphemism for the State of Israel, so this clause in fact calls for the destruction of Israel, not just the end of Zionism.

Where subtleties in the original Arabic are important, the Arabic word has been inserted in parentheses.

The Palestinian National Charter is a good example of how lazy people are inclined to believe others and they will follow them to Hell.

THE PALESTINIAN NATIONAL CHARTER:
Resolutions of the Palestine National Council,
July 1-17, 1968
Text of the Charter:

Article 1: Palestine is the homeland of the Arab Palestinian people; it is an indivisible part of the Arab homeland, and the Palestinian people are an integral part of the Arab nation.

Article 2: Palestine, with the boundaries it had during the British Mandate, is an indivisible territorial unit.

Article 3: The Palestinian Arab people possess the legal right to their homeland and have the right to determine their destiny after achieving the liberation of their country in accordance with their wishes and entirely of their own accord and will.

Article 4: The Palestinian identity is a genuine, essential, and inherent characteristic; it is transmitted from parents to children. The Zionist occupation and the dispersal of the Palestinian Arab people, through the disasters which befell them, do not make them lose their Palestinian identity and their membership in the Palestinian community, nor do they negate them.

Article 5: The Palestinians are those Arab nationals who, until 1947, normally resided in Palestine regardless of whether they were evicted from it or have stayed there. Anyone born, after that date, of a Palestinian father - whether inside Palestine or outside it - is also a Palestinian.

Article 6: The Jews who had normally resided in Palestine until the beginning of the Zionist invasion will be considered Palestinians.

Article 7: That there is a Palestinian community and that it has material, spiritual, and historical connection with Palestine are indisputable facts. It is a national duty to bring up individual Palestinians in an Arab revolutionary manner. All means of information and education must be adopted in order to acquaint the Palestinian with his country in the most profound manner, both spiritual and material, that is possible. He must be prepared for the armed struggle and ready to sacrifice his wealth and his life in order to win back his homeland and bring about its liberation.

Article 8: The phase in their history, through which the Palestinian people are now living, is that of national (watani) struggle for the liberation of Palestine. Thus the conflicts among the Palestinian national forces are secondary, and should be ended for the sake of the basic conflict that exists between the forces of Zionism and of imperialism on the one hand, and the Palestinian Arab people on the other. On this basis the Palestinian masses, regardless of whether they are residing in the national homeland or in diaspora (mahajir) constitute - both their organizations and the individuals - one national front working for the retrieval of Palestine and its liberation through armed struggle.

Article 9: Armed struggle is the only way to liberate Palestine. Thus it is the overall strategy, not merely a tactical phase. The Palestinian Arab people assert their absolute determination and firm resolution to continue their armed struggle and to work for an armed popular revolution for the liberation of their country and their return to it. They also assert their right to normal life in Palestine and to exercise their right to self-determination and sovereignty over it.

Article 10: Commando action constitutes the nucleus of the Palestinian popular liberation war. This requires its escalation, comprehensiveness, and the mobilization of all the Palestinian popular and educational efforts and their organization and involvement in the armed Palestinian revolution. It also requires the achieving of unity for the national (watani) struggle among the different groupings of the Palestinian people, and between the Palestinian people and the Arab masses, so as to secure the continuation of the revolution, its escalation, and victory.

Article 11: The Palestinians will have three mottoes: national (wataniyya) unity, national (qawmiyya) mobilization, and liberation

Article 12: The Palestinian people believe in Arab unity. In order to contribute their share toward the attainment of that objective, however, they must, at the present stage of their struggle, safeguard their Palestinian identity and develop their consciousness of that identity, and oppose any plan that may dissolve or impair it.

Article 13: Arab unity and the liberation of Palestine are two complementary objectives, the attainment of either of which facilitates the attainment of the other. Thus, Arab unity leads to the liberation of Palestine, the liberation of Palestine leads to Arab unity; and work toward the realization of one objective proceeds side by side with work toward the realization of the other.

Article 14: The destiny of the Arab nation, and indeed Arab existence itself, depend upon the destiny of the Palestine cause. From this interdependence springs the Arab nation's pursuit of, and striving for, the liberation of Palestine. The people of Palestine play the role of the vanguard in the realization of this sacred (qawmi) goal.

Article 15: The liberation of Palestine, from an Arab viewpoint, is a national (qawmi) duty and it attempts to repel the Zionist and imperialist aggression against the Arab homeland, and aims at the elimination of Zionism in Palestine. Absolute responsibility for this falls upon the Arab nation - peoples and governments - with the Arab people of Palestine in the vanguard. Accordingly, the Arab nation must mobilize all its military, human, moral, and spiritual capabilities to participate actively with the Palestinian people in the liberation of

Palestine. It must, particularly in the phase of the armed Palestinian revolution, offer and furnish the Palestinian people with all possible help, and material and human support, and make available to them the means and opportunities that will enable them to continue to carry out their leading role in the armed revolution, until they liberate their homeland.

Article 16: The liberation of Palestine, from a spiritual point of view, will provide the Holy Land with an atmosphere of safety and tranquility, which in turn will safeguard the country's religious sanctuaries and guarantee freedom of worship and of visit to all, without discrimination of race, color, language, or religion. Accordingly, the people of Palestine look to all spiritual forces in the world for support.

Article 17: The liberation of Palestine, from a human point of view, will restore to the Palestinian individual his dignity, pride, and freedom. Accordingly the Palestinian Arab people look forward to the support of all those who believe in the dignity of man and his freedom in the world.

Article 18: The liberation of Palestine, from an international point of view, is a defensive action necessitated by the demands of self-defense. Accordingly the Palestinian people, desirous as they are of the friendship of all people, look to freedom-loving, and peace-loving states for support in order to restore their legitimate rights in Palestine, to re-establish peace and security in the country, and to enable its people to exercise national sovereignty and freedom.

Article 19: The partition of Palestine in 1947 and the establishment of the state of Israel are entirely illegal, regardless of the passage of time, because they were contrary to the will of the Palestinian people and to their natural right in their homeland, and inconsistent with the principles embodied in the Charter of the United Nations, particularly the right to self-determination.

Article 20: The Balfour Declaration, the Mandate for Palestine, and everything that has been based upon them, are deemed null and void. Claims of historical or religious ties of Jews with Palestine are incompatible with the facts of history and the true conception of what constitutes statehood. Judaism, being a religion, is not an independent nationality. Nor do Jews constitute a single nation with an identity of its own; they are citizens of the states to which they belong.

Article 21: The Arab Palestinian people, expressing themselves by the armed Palestinian revolution, reject all solutions which are substitutes for the total liberation of Palestine and reject all proposals aiming at the liquidation of the Palestinian problem, or its internationalization.

Article 22: Zionism is a political movement organically associated with international imperialism and antagonistic to all action for liberation and to progressive movements in the world. It is racist and fanatic in its nature, aggressive, expansionist, and colonial in its aims, and fascist in its methods. Israel is the instrument of the Zionist movement, and geographical base for world imperialism placed strategically in the midst of the Arab homeland to combat the hopes of the Arab nation for liberation, unity, and progress. Israel is a constant source of threat vis-a-vis peace in the Middle East and the whole world. Since the liberation of Palestine will destroy the Zionist and imperialist presence and will contribute to the establishment of peace in the Middle East, the Palestinian people look for the support of all the progressive and peaceful forces and urge them all, irrespective of their affiliations and beliefs, to offer the Palestinian people all aid and support in their just struggle for the liberation of their homeland.

Article 23: The demand of security and peace, as well as the demand of right and justice, require all states to consider Zionism an illegitimate movement, to outlaw its existence, and to ban its operations, in order that friendly relations among peoples may be preserved, and the loyalty of citizens to their respective homelands safeguarded.

Article 24: The Palestinian people believe in the principles of justice, freedom, sovereignty, self-determination, human dignity, and in the right of all peoples to exercise them.

Article 25: For the realization of the goals of this Charter and its principles, the Palestine Liberation Organization will perform its role in the liberation of Palestine in accordance with the Constitution of this Organization.

Article 26: The Palestine Liberation Organization, representative of the Palestinian revolutionary forces, is responsible for the

Palestinian Arab people's movement in its struggle - to retrieve its homeland, liberate and return to it and exercise the right to self-determination in it - in all military, political, and financial fields and also for whatever may be required by the Palestine case on the inter-Arab and international levels.

Article 27: The Palestine Liberation Organization shall cooperate with all Arab states, each according to its potentialities; and will adopt a neutral policy among them in the light of the requirements of the war of liberation; and on this basis it shall not interfere in the internal affairs of any Arab state.

Article 28: The Palestinian Arab people assert the genuineness and independence of their national (wataniyya) revolution and reject all forms of intervention, trusteeship, and subordination.

Article 29: The Palestinian people possess the fundamental and genuine legal right to liberate and retrieve their homeland. The Palestinian people determine their attitude toward all states and forces on the basis of the stands they adopt vis-a-vis to the Palestinian revolution to fulfill the aims of the Palestinian people.

Article 30: Fighters and carriers of arms in the war of liberation are the nucleus of the popular army which will be the protective force for the gains of the Palestinian Arab people.

Article 31: The Organization shall have a flag, an oath of allegiance, and an anthem. All this shall be decided upon in accordance with a special regulation.

Article 32: Regulations, which shall be known as the Constitution of the Palestinian Liberation Organization, shall be annexed to this Charter. It will lay down the manner in which the Organization, and its organs and institutions, shall be constituted; the respective competence of each; and the requirements of its obligation under the Charter.

Article 33: This Charter shall not be amended save by [vote of] a majority of two-thirds of the total membership of the National Congress of the Palestine Liberation Organization [taken] at a special session convened for that purpose.

Do you think Arafat or Muhammad or the Palestinians are in any other place than Hell?

Islam is not the only evil force in the world, and to help you understand other Sins of humans, think of Adultery and Divorce.

And the Angel Jo said to David, "When I was in body and during 1965, you and I had a summer love affair. It was good for you, for you needed it to be where you are today, and yet, it was wrong because we were both married to another at the time.

"Divorce does not come to two people that travel in the same direction. One must change direction from the other to ever consider divorce. But also, divorce may come to couples who were not traveling in the same directions when they married. But also, one can be deceived by another before marriage. Therefore, it is not always a Sin to divorce, because if one has Sinned, and if he deceives or lies to the other before they marry, then they must divorce. Both will be judge by God as one. If one stays with another when the other is Sinning, they both say that the other is correct with his actions and those actions are against their children. And it is not unusual for one to seek love from another while married, for humans are still animals that contain its individual desires. But it is a Sin to judge what another has done, because God has given you the Knowledge not to judge another. For you do not know the reasons of why of another' action and all actions are interwoven into life.

"The Hell that people live in today, may not be their Hells of tomorrow. Everyone is in the exact place in time that they are supposed to be. If they repent, and change their views of the past, they may be in their Heaven today. One should not judge others' for their life but only their actions should be judged to see if they are correct for you.

"Adultery in today's terms means; having sexual involvement with another other than your spouse.

"Once one marries, the two become one in the eyes of God. If two are one and if one half turns on its other half, is that not the same as one divided and seeking good while enjoying evil at the same time?

"If a marriage has eroded to a depth of no love, then, divorce is imminent because of a love that has been lost may be obtained from another. For a marriage that contains Adultery places many people, including their children, in Hell.

"What constitutes marriage?

"A piece of paper or the coming together of two people in the eyes of God?

"What length of time do the Christians say two people should be together before God proclaims their marriage?

"' Til death do us part, is what Christians say, but what about after life?

"Does a Christian seek God while he enjoys hearing about others in Adultery?

"Is refusing entry to an Adulteress into God's House not placing one's self above God and enjoying it?

"No one has the right to refuse another entry into God's House, only their houses.

"Can one that has committed Adultery not repent?

"Divorce is not right, but sometimes things must happen before one can be at a given point at a certain time. Therefore, people should not judge why a person does things as they head for a certain point in a given time, for they do not know the Master Plan. And if God judged you for your past, I would surely not be talking with you, but your past was needed by you.

"Adultery with many should never happen, but if Adultery occurs with one while you are still married to another, you will or will not repent, but your decision should not be based on what others say, it should come from your heart as you seek God. "

Then Jesus said unto me, "Husband and wife shall stand in front of God to be Judged as one.

"The time that a man and woman are together, God shall Judge them as one."

Think of that... Whenever a man and a woman marry... join together, they become one in their actions and directions of life, therefore they shall be judged as one because each one allows and/or agrees with all the other does and all that each one owns becomes part of what the other owns and for that the other owns also becomes part of what each one owns. For they are now one. Is that not different for Bill and Hilary.

And Jesus continued, "Marriage is not just for making BABIES nor is it for the lust of beauty or to become rich in earth-goods. For the body will wither away and return to the dirt of which it came from and the concept of life that you have placed into your offspring will remain for another lifetime. Therefore, not only will husband and wife be judged as one but also husband and wife SHALL be judged for what they taught and allowed their children to do for parents have control over their children's actions.

"Marriage is a partnership between a man and a woman. Each one to agree on all actions of their partner.

"Marriage is not slavery of one to the other.

"Marriage is the same as any business partnership for the good of each partner and the human race. But it is wrong to divorce because one grows old and is not as beautiful as when one married and it is not okay to divorce because your spouse cannot give you children.

"Do not court under false attitude and do not try to force one's beliefs unto another, even one's spouse or future spouse. But it is okay to leave and divorce one that does not or will not live as God wishes us to live - a righteous life."

(This is not just belief in God or religion but all other beliefs such as paying bills, lying, stealing, living in a dirty house, not working, controlling or dominating people and other things.)

And Jesus continued, "Do not allow another to place you in domination and do not place yourself in self-domination for another, for both are the Sin that you will be committing.

"Do not allow your parents or others to control or dominate you after you turn of age. Before you turn of age, your parents are to teach (inspire) you to live the correct way of life. If they do not then that is their "Hell" and not yours but remove yourself from them when you become of age.

"Allowing others to force you into judging yourself, them or others, is allowing them to place you in self-domination. Turn the other cheek, for that cheek has not been contaminated by them."

Recently David finished a short trip across part of the U.S. and have found that most people ask him the same question; What does God or Jesus say about Adultery and divorce?

And the Angel Jo said, "Christians say of those who are not Christian; If they, the Christian, do wrong, it is a Sin. And yet, they say, 'If a Christian does wrong, he has only back-slid.' And they also say, 'If one, who has a sexual affair and is not married, he is running around.' And they say; 'If a person is married and is sleeping with another, he is committing Adultery.'

"Sin is doing something that you <u>know</u> is wrong, and not what you <u>think</u> is wrong. A Christian doing something wrong is committing Sin, for he knows that it is wrong. A person who is married and sleeps with others is doing something wrong, for he too, knows it is wrong - it is Adultery. The animal merely <u>thinks</u> of what he is doing and never <u>knows</u> what he is doing.

"Does your minister or preacher use the word 'think' or 'know' when he talks?

"How about your friends?

"These words truly show where they stand with God.

"In the story of Adam and Eve, they did not have the Knowledge until God told them, 'Do not eat from this tree.' God knew exactly what Adam and Eve would do. (But up until that point, they were merely animals and like those Christians who say they know who is a Sinner.) But once God told them not to eat from that tree, then, they were human and above animals, for they had the Knowledge, too.

"The biggest problem with humans, they can only comprehend in the realty that they live, and they always say they know what God thinks.

"The Knowledge that Adam and Eve were inspired by God to learn, was that He had forbidden them to eat from that tree, that tree was the tree of Knowledge. What people could not understand, it was the knowledge that separates humans from animals, but people say, 'Eve committed the first Sin.' If Eve committed Sin after she had knowledge of God, then did not she just back-slide?

"And if she did, and if all Christians who have done wrong, have in fact, she did nothing more than committing the Sin – back-slide, as all Christians claim they do.

"And yet, Christians place themselves higher than others. They do not judge themselves or others in their group as Sinners, but they will judge others outside of their group as Sinners.

"If a Christian who has Sinned other than Adultery, people in his group will say, 'he has only back-slid,' but one who commits Adultery cannot be part of their group. Therefore, this group of Christians will ban the adulterer from their group and church. And yet, Christians worship Jesus as their God, and claim they follow His teachings. But did He ban anyone from His group?

"Is it not their church but God's?

"Who did Jesus teach?

"Who do We - God's Angels teach?

"The righteous do not need teaching, the sinner does.

"Should not the sinner be welcomed into God's House?

"Should not the stronger help the weaker?

"Repentance - changing your ideas from what they were in the past into thoughts that should include <u>God,</u> is the help the stronger should give to the weaker. But also, one can repent to the negative. For the stronger will teach to inspire the weaker, for then, the weaker become the stronger and can help or hurt others, too. Inasmuch, a stronger negative can inspire a weaker positive into evil – negative and Hell."

Many "born again Christians" say that David is in communication with Satan. Because Satan can be deceitful and can present himself as God or God's Angels. But his answer to them is: in their Bible it says, ask the Angel that approaches you, if he is of God. For even Satan must tell you the truth. And also, we know the difference between right and wrong. So if an Angel tells you to do something that is wrong, then he is of Satan, and demand him to leave and he will.

Now, let's continue understanding things in the world, that will place a person in Hell.

After Jesus was murdered, his half brother, James, took up the position as Bishop over Jesus' Ministry. Then, Paul and Simon Peter headed toward Rome while preaching the "Good News" of Jesus' Death along the way. Stop and think for a minute, how can anyone's death be Good News?

Almost 100 % of Christians that have died are in Hell. The following is another great story that explains some of the ideas of Christianity.

Most think that Simon Peter was the first leader, Bishop of the old Roman Church that is now known as the Roman Catholic Church, but Simon Peter actually reported back to James in Jerusalem while Paul just kept preaching. Therefore, James was the first leader of the church after Jesus died.

When Simon Peter was crucified, he asked to be hung upside down because was not as worthy as Jesus, thus he died on the cross upside down. He requested this because of the faith and belief that he held in Jesus being the Son of God, and not as Jesus being Lord.

(Incidentally for the true record, James was thrown to his death in 62AD.)

Over the next few hundred years, people thought of Heaven as a great meal or dinner. And during this time, communal dinners or suppers were held in individual homes where the woman of the house led the Christian Services. Services were held this way so that the Roman Soldiers did not see them as being Christian Services and would not jail or kill the participants. But once again, Faith and Belief in Jesus and in God caused them to hold Services, even though they knew that if they were found out, they would be killed.

It was during the second hundred years after Jesus died that his Ministry, now called Christianity took on the order and/or ranks as the Roman Empire, which has one person at the top with the Bishops and Deacons and others below. Also at this time, the Church stopped women from conducting and/or leading Services in their homes.

300 AD, the Roman Empire split in two parts - the east and the west and was falling apart.

Constantine was placed in charge of the area that we now call England. Constantine decided that he wanted to be the Emperor over the complete Roman Empire and thought that he could pull it back together again. As he fought and won his battles across the Roman Empire and while he was 13 miles outside of Rome and just before a battle at a bridge, he looked up and saw a cross on the sun and heard a voice say, "You are to conquer under this sign."

He immediately had his men paint crosses on their shields and then, he flew a banner that contained a cross as they entered into the battle and won. He then, went on and defeated the eastern part of the Roman Empire under the cross and thus, brought the western and eastern parts back together, re-uniting them once again. Now Constantine was Emperor over the complete Roman Empire.

Constantine's newly found Faith if God and Jesus caused him to bring the Empire back together. And he adopted Christianity as the Religion of the Roman Empire. But soon, many new beliefs and doctrines on Christianity started to appear. And in 325 AD, his Faith and Belief in Jesus and God made him call Church leaders together to decide what day should be celebrated as Easter. And it was during that meeting, the Trinity - the Father, Son and Holy Ghost being one, as we know it today was conceived. Also, they canonized the Christian Bible - they put together the Bible stories that are pretty well the same as those that are in the present day Christian Bible, but many other stories were changed while others were left out.

This meeting and finalizing - the canonizing of the Bible, was to keep the east and west parts of the Roman Empire, the known world, together under one Emperor - Constantine, and also to keep the Church in step with him. After this meeting, Constantine ordered 50 Bibles to be printed (written by hand) so that it could never be changed.

Later, Constantine moved the capital of Rome to the city that we know as Istanbul - Constantinople.

In 440 AD, Leo the first, was elected as the Bishop of Rome. He declared one Bishop over all the others and proclaims his title as Pope. The title "Pope" came from the people calling the Bishop of their towns "Papa" and that was translated into "Pope."

With the capital of Rome moving east, the western part of the Empire and the city of Rome was left to fend for themselves. And in 452 AD, after Rome had been sacked by many different groups, Attila the Hun camped near Rome and waited for daylight to sack and destroy Rome. Leo the first, walked upon the hillside to Attila the Hun's camp and there beside him appeared the Angels of Peter and Paul, both with swords in their hands. The Angels said to Attila the Hun, "Do not enter Rome or you will be slain." The next morning Attila the Hun was gone.

The belief of Attila the Hun, one of history's most brutal warriors, one who killed his own brother to become ruler over his kingdom, after seeing the two Angels of Simon Peter and Paul, made him leave without a fight. Did he truly believe in God?

In the 700s AD, Muhammad came back from the desert and told his wife that he had been talking with God and that if he told anyone else, they would think he was insane. She persuaded him to tell others, and soon his Islamic Religion spread across part of the known world. But he listened to her because he believed in the Torah.

After Muhammad's death, his followers began using the sword to convert people. For if they did not convert to the Islamic Religion, they would be killed. But it did not matter if they truly believed or not because their children were brain-washed into believing in

Muhammad.

Around 1,000 AD the Crusades began because the Muslims had taken over Jerusalem and would not allow Christians or any people of other religions entry into the city. During this time in history, all Christians had to journey to Jerusalem at least once in their lives. Therefore, the Crusades were to liberate Jerusalem. And it was during the first Christian Crusade, many stories were told and recorded in history, about Christian soldiers that were slain in battle, would get back up and continue to fight. They won, and Christianity ruled over Jerusalem, but once again the Muslims fought back and recaptured the city. Then, over the next two hundreds years, the next five Crusades occurred. The 5th Crusade was the Children's Crusade, all but the first failed because only the first was for God, the other 5 were for man - the dog, and where the Christian men beat down their Christian children from their Crusade.

Let's move on in history to the 1,400s. At the age of 13, Joan of Arc received a message from the Angel Michael to re-unite the French and Charles VII. Her Faith in God caused her to lead an army and win many battles that proclaimed Charles VII as King of France. And that was all that she was instructed to do, but she thought that God wanted more and continued to fight on, but lost all the battles from that point on, and was burned at the stake on May 30th, 1431.

Why did Joan fail?

Because she thought she knew what God wanted. But He only wanted her to lead the battle to put Charles the VII on the throne, not any more.

If you refer back to the New Testament, Jesus is standing near a cliff and Satan is talking to him. Satan said something like, "Jump, your Father will save you."

Jesus replied, "I will not tempt God."

(For years, David did not understand what "tempt" meant until the Angels explained it this way. Tempt means to coax, to persuade, but is still a demand and that is domination. And God will not allow anyone or anything to dominate Him. Therefore, when Joan of Arc continued to battle after her mission was completed, she was then trying to demand God's help. And that is exactly what many of us expect from our prayers.)

But back to Joan of Arc, can you imagine how much Faith and Belief that Charles and the French people had in her and in God to allow her - an 18 or 19 year old girl to lead their army into battle. And how much Faith she had in God to approach Charles with her plan! Her "Peace of Mind is Worth the Truth" in the Christian God caused her to place her beliefs into Hell.

During 1912, C. Austin Miles wrote the words and music to "In The Garden" after experiencing a vision of Mary Magdalene weeping at Jesus' Tomb and when Mary saw Jesus standing there, she knelt before him with arms outstretched and cried, "Rabboni," meaning "My Lord! My Master."

And this thought placed people's concepts of Jesus being the Lord in Hell.

All these stories that are mentioned contained Faith and Belief by people throughout history. Their stories cannot be denied. Each one of them had visions and/or heard voices from Heaven telling them something that needed to be done. Should it be any different today.

But you decide who went to Heaven or Hell.

We try to inspire others to find God as the Angels inspired David. Therefore, the Angels call him a Guider; for he help others seek their god as he guide others toward the one God. It does not matter which god you follow as long as your religion says to love all and have no domination toward others, you will do fine.

The following are of others beliefs that have placed many in Hell because hearing others say things that they like is "Peace of Mind is Worth the Truth".

All through the years of his ministry Jessie Jackson tried to act in a God like way, posing as if he does not sin and that he does not act like all other humans. Around 22 months ago, Jessie talked with Bill Clinton about coming clean to the public about his affairs with different women. Yet at the same time Jessie was having a sexual affair with a young woman outside of his marriage and who worked under Jessie Jackson in his Rainbow Coalition, and they created life, a baby. The only way this story broke and Jessie admitted to his sinful actions was because a tabloid found out and was going to run the story in its newspaper. The Jessie Jackson's Sinful Affair story was announced to the public around the same day that Bill Clinton confessed to lying under oath about his Sinful affairs.

Now we move on to the story of Bill Clinton perjury - giving false statements about his sexual conduct while under oath only cost him a fine of $25,000 and he could not practice law for 5 years. His admitted guilt came too late for him to be impeached. Bill Clinton knew exactly what he was doing (lying to the people of the country that he took an oath to uphold and protect the truth,) and disregarded all that the office of President of the United States holds dear. Bill Clinton planned his admittance in the same manner as killer plans his attack upon his prey.

One question for you to answer; in your opinion did the Vise President Gore and Bill's wife, Hilary, know what was going on?

Now we come to Hilary.

She stood by Bill throughout his years in the office as President of the United States. Did she know the truth through the past months?

Or did Bill also lie to her?

He is known to have run around on Hilary for many years before he was President?

Could she have not known about his extra marital affairs during his presidency?

Is Hilary also a liar?

Hilary was just voted in as Senator of New York state. Will she lie in the Senate as a Senator, too?

If she lied to the people about her husband, will she not lie to the people as a Senator?

What should Hilary do now?

Should she divorce Bill?

If she stays married to him, she is approving of all that he has done including the lying that he has done to the people let alone to her. Can the people trust a person who is married to a known liar?

You need to remember for someday she will run for President of the U.S, but she would make a better President than the Muslim.

And the Angel Jo said unto David, "No matter what happens, Islam is needed in the world."

And David's question is when did Bill Clinton first tell them about his lustful actions?

When Jessie Jackson talked with Bill Clinton and begged Bill to come clean with the people about his affairs some 22 months ago, he too was lying to the people. Will we ever know for sure if Jessie was told by Bill about his affairs at that time or were they discussing who of them were the better lover?

But we do know that Jessie Jackson was finally pinned down by a tabloid, confessed his affair and fathered a child 20 some months ago out of his marriage and it is reported that he paid the woman $40,000 to move and $3,000 per month for child support. And I understand that the Rainbow Coalition is paying her $10,000 per month too.

Another question for you is, where does Jessie Jackson get his money?

Where is the Rainbow Coalition getting its money from?

Who is really paying for Jessie Jackson's mistakes?

Oh yes, Jessie stated he will stay out of the spot light for some time. Boy what a punishment he placed upon himself.

But let's get to the point of all of this.

We are all humans. We all made and will make mistakes. It's okay to make mistakes but also we must be able to admit to our mistakes - confess what we have done wrongly and do not do it again. We are not Jesus or God. Bill and Jessie were trying to act Godly when they refused to admit their mistakes when they happened. They only admitted what they had done when they were pinned down. This waiting until there was no way out for them shows they cannot be trusted or believed in. Therefore from now on, no matter what these three people say or do, David will not believe it or in them. They have lost face not only with God but with the people, too. God may forgive them. But we do not have to forgive them, that is one of the choices that God has given us. David will never forgive them. That is his choice as given to him from God. David, too, made mistakes. He is human. He admits that he is human. He was Ordained as a Bishop and a Prophet of God by God, but he is still human. Do not look upon him as being any closer to God or more Godly than you, he is not. He am just a human trying to pass on to you what the Angels have told him.

Do you really think that all those people who's lives were written into the Bible did nothing wrong?

The Bible only reported of the things that made people look more Righteous than us, that's all. All the people in the Bible stories were just human, too.

Anytime that you place yourself in the spot light, people will be watching you closely. They will be watching for your mistakes. If you are in the spot light, admit that you are human and that you must try not to make mistakes but when you do, admit your mistakes and go on. You cannot hide them forever, they will come back to haunt you later.

David smokes about 2 packs of cigarettes daily but if that is a sin, what about driving an automobile?

The cigarettes that he smokes do place pollution into his body, but what about the pollution from cars that others put into our air daily?

They not only put pollution into our bodies but also sre they not putting polluted air into all the people that breathe, and share the air?

Are we, the people who drive and use automobiles not placing our sin of using automobiles above and on others, including the ones who smoke cigarettes?

Are our sins less then our brother's?

Can we and should we judge others before we judge ourselves?

Clean your house first before you come down on David for his smoking of cigarettes.

Smoking does NOT cause cancer, all the other chemicals that we place in our bodies does that.

If you come into a spot light such as our newly elected President Bush, you, as he, must confess your past mistakes, and you should not make them again. President Bush's past mistakes just as with our past mistakes has made us all what we are today. Those things of our past allowed us to grow into what we are today.

We should forgive ourselves and others for past mistakes, but we cannot keep forgiving if the same mistake continue to happen to an individual. Jessie Jackson and Bill Clinton continued by lying and not admitting their mistakes for over 20 months. Hilary knew of Bill's mistake but refused to tell of them because of the position that she wanted to obtain, Senator of New York.

Jessie Jackson has delivered a slap to all clergymen and all black people for his actions.

Bill Clinton has delivered a slap to all Americans and to all males for his actions.

Hilary continues to deliver slaps to all people of all races and not in just the Untied States, but in every part and place in the world for her actions.

David will <u>never</u> trust Jessie Jackson, Bill Clinton or Hilary again, will you?

Here are a few other Hells that peers place others in, including their children.

A certain elderly man, who is a billionaire stated to me that when he was born, he was so ugly that his father just knew God was punishing him for marrying a woman 25 years his junior and his parents did not have any other children because of his ugliness.

This certain man was not born into a rich family and yet, this ugly son grew up into a great wealthy man, who employed many that he has helped over the years. Yes, he may have only helped others by giving them employment, but their jobs put food in their mouths, and money into his banking accounts, that raised families with many wonderful children that came from those he employed. But, even him, do you think he will live in Heaven forever?

Another good example of peer pressure is a couple that are friends of mine, she is an Afro-American and he is of Islamic decent, conceived a child while living together out of wedlock and during the last weeks of her pregnancy the unborn child died. The man's mother who did not accept their relationship stated that she was the cause for the child's death because her god was angry at her for not accepting the Afro-American woman being with her son.

It is inconceivable to think that any person would believe God would place punishment onto an unborn or newly born baby for the child did nothing wrong in the eyes of God, so why would any person think God would punish another for his or her mistakes or Sins (wrong doings)?

Any person who thinks the physical appearance, abilities and/or the mental condition of their offspring is their punishment from God are completely wrong for they do not know God. God does not punish one by inflicting something upon another. Those who think such things as that are in fact, placing themselves above their offspring and yet, all people are created equal.

Ignorant people believe everything, including the thoughts of God, belongs to them. They think all life that surrounds them is for their personal needs and wants. How stupid it is for any human to think God looks at them alone. But people only know of God by the corrupted words spoken by their preacher referring to a polluted Bible.

We are to inspire (rise up) all others around us into following a righteous life style. One should inspire his or her spouse into wanting a better life. Do not stand beside one who tries to control or dominate you or others. For all people are equal.

Do unto others as they do unto you - If the Love you give is not returned but instead you receive back a slap, then it is okay to walk away from the other. A Love for a Love and a slap for a slap.

Do not lower your values for another.

Do not place yourself in Hell for anyone.

To live a righteous life one needs not know of the 10 Commandments or of God and not belong to any religious group but only treat others as you wish to be treated. Then you have found your Salvation to God and everlasting life.

At approximately 5:30AM on February 23rd of this year, a man jumped to his death from one of the twin towers of a hotel located in Los Angeles, California.

David's last story of causes of Hell came from the Police and Coroner who worked on their task of a suicide scene, the "ghost" of the dead man drifted unseen as if he were smoke around and over his broken human body. For now he knew that the things in his life that caused him to commit suicide were futile and that he only released himself from human life and placed himself in an everlasting Hell of true reality.

This 45 year old man checked into the motel in February, and it is believed that he spent most of the last two weeks of his life dwelling on suicide.

When his room was inspected, the police found everything very neat and a note that he had left for them. The note said in part; I have taken my life... you are not responsible... I loved you... give my things to my son. His note also contained the phone number of his ex-wife.

This man who committed suicide thought there was nothing in this world worth living for - his elderly mother and father... his twelve year old son who he cared enough about to give all his belongs to...

During his two week stay in the motel, this man spent most of his time watching movies on television and drinking beer, so he must have liked movies and beer, yet these things and his family were still not enough for him to live. Yet, he had a good job for he had a credit card that he was able to charge his room on. But for whatever reason he thought his life was not worth living.

This guy who jumped, did not think that his littlest actions or movements were worth living for. How can one not like or enjoy one little thing in one's life?

This man, who jumped from the motel, now drifts in Hell until the end of time when God will judge him for his actions of self-center feelings - his selfishness.

David is truly sad for his son and his elderly mother and father.

May God forgive him for what he has done to others. How can anyone not have one thing to live for?

Look at what the people who lived and died in the Second World War endured. Think about what Hitler put the Jews and others through. Think of them starving, freezing and enduring some of the worst treatment ever delivered from man unto man, yet they did not commit suicide. The little they had was enough for them to live another day. But this 45 year old man, who lived in the United States of America in the year of 2001, did not think his life was worth living. How sad, for the demands we place upon ourselves and others.

Blasphemes of the Father and/or of the Son may be forgiven on Earth and in Heaven.

Blasphemes against the Holy Spirit are not forgiven on Earth or in Heaven.

Suicide is Blaspheme against the Holy Spirit.

This man that jumped, committed Blaspheme against the Holy Spirit. He made a statement with his act of suicide that said, "Nothing that God has created is worth living for."

That is saying all that God has created is wrong and worthless.

The Holy Spirit means; the ideas, concept and thoughts of God. Therefore, one could say God's Holy Spirit is Life. When this man took his life, he was saying God's Spirit of Life is not worth living.

During my youth, I never really thought about death but in the mid-80s, David came down with Epstein Barr Virus, now known as Yuppie Flu. He was disabled for around ten months and it was then when he started thinking about death and the "Quality of Life." He thought when his life was no longer what he would consider quality, he would just commit suicide. Well, you know that time never came.

Even today, he sometimes has the symptoms of EB Virus along with the pains he frequently gets from his heart condition but those, even though sometimes they are great, are not enough for him to consider suicide.

The disabled person, who cannot move part of his body still has quality of life. The person laying in a coma and dying from cancer, and who is cared for 24 hours a day by his family members still has quality of life.

David has learned that the final breath that we take before God and nature takes our lives away is quality of life and worth the other pains and hurts that we endure.

On a daily basis, rather you know it or not, each one of us enjoys thousands of things. Each day we decide what is right or wrong for us, that is deciding of things we like or dislike. (I do not want to list every little thing that you or I do daily, but think about your movements and things you do daily.)

In Genesis of the Christian Bible it talks about being aware that if you walk up the steps and stand on an Altar, people may look up under your skirt and see your nakedness.

In translation that means; if you stand up in front of people and pose as being better than others and/or if you try to act in a God like way, people may see that you are only human. Repent, change your views of the past, you still have time to place your Soul in Heaven.

A long time ago a man named Jesus talked to some men about his ideas of God. These men, his disciples, could not understand just what he was talking about and kept asking him questions.

Jesus knew that only a part of what he was trying to teach them was being absorbed, but he kept repeating over and over again his messages of Love to them.

When Jesus' death became imminent, though he knew his followers did not completely understand what he had told them, he instructed them to go out in different directions and to tell others about his ideas of God.

After Jesus was murdered, His followers did what He had told them do to.

From the death of Jesus until around 75 AD, Jesus' disciples had scribes write His stories in their individual words down and then years later most of these stories along with many writings about God were destroyed by fire.

Roughly around 50 AD, one of Jesus' disciples, named Peter, went to Rome and after telling some people of the "good news," he was killed because his teachings went against Rome's religion of that time.

For the next hundred to two hundred or so years, the people that listened to others telling the stories what Peter once told were persecuted by the Romans and many were put to death for their beliefs.

Around 300 AD, a "Ruler" of Rome in battle had a vision that he claimed helped him win the battle and war, and he changed the ideas of Rome and declared that this little known cult of Christianity was now the Religion of Rome.

Over the next few years, Christianity spread across Rome. But soon the Roman Empire started to divide because the two capitals of the Roman Empire, the east and the west capitals, both wanted to be the center of Christianity and claim the true Church of Rome.

This "Ruler" of Rome, who proclaimed Christianity as Rome's Religion, decided to set up a book (Bible) that would be the laws and rules for the Church of Rome, and that would place the city of Rome as the center for the Church of Rome. Thus, he would keep control over the complete Empire of Rome - the total known world.

It was at this time a meeting between Church Leaders was set up by this Roman "Ruler." After a few days of discussion of what should be included and what should be removed from their religion, this Ruler put a time limit to complete "his" Bible. The Church Leaders then hastily placed different stories together and created the Christian Bible. The Roman "Ruler" then proclaimed - Canonize the Bible. From that point in time the Bible, God and Jesus were as if set in stone and never changed again.

Around the 17th century, some of the original stories were removed from our present day Catholic Bible. Also from the 17th century to present day, many different branches of Christian Religion sprang forth from the Catholic Religion, which was the original Church of Rome.

Today Christian Theology still uses the writings of the old Church of Rome as the Gospel. Yet most Christians say the Catholic Religion is polluted and corrupted.

Human pride caused the old Church of Rome Leaders during the time that the Bible was Canonized, to believe everything that they claimed to be of God as the truth.

Human pride caused those who removed stories from the Bible during the 17th century to believe they only removed from the Bible those things that were not true.

Human pride caused the people who started the different Christian Religions in the 17th century to present day to believe their Religion was the true Religion of God.

Human pride causes the people who start Religions today to believe their Religion is the true Religion of God. Did not James Jones also think he was following God?

People of any and all Religions believe they know how and what God's ideas and thoughts are. It is human pride that causes the "born again Christians" to become defensive if you confront them with these questions;

"How do you know how God thinks?"

"How do you know what God looks like?"

"How do you know what color God is?"

"Why do you worship Jesus instead of God?

"There is but one Lord above all, and that Lord is God."

The study of religion is called <u>Theology</u>. Theology means the study of religion, culminating in a synthesis or philosophy of religion.

The word <u>"Philosophy"</u> means the inquiry into the principles of reality in general, or of some sector of it, as <u>human knowledge</u> or <u>human values.</u>

Therefore, people who study God in human concepts are corrupting God's Words.

Most of the documented statements from Jesus were mis-translated by his disciples. And then his disciples' statements were polluted with their individual thoughts and ideas and also were mis-translated by the scribes. Most of these and other religious records were destroyed by fire long ago. Then the Church of Rome threw out many stories when they created the Christian Bible. Later others removed things that they did not believe in, so how in the world can Theology be a true study or understanding of God?

Human pride of what humans think they know drives them down

into Hell, for human pride places man beside or above God.

There is no way humans can know what God thinks or His ideas just by reading the Bible. We cannot think in His dimension. Nor can we know for sure what was the actual words used in conversations between God and humans or Jesus and his followers just by reading the Bible. By reading the Bible all we can only be sure about is the ideas or spirit of what is said in the Bible that we know.

Therefore, read the Bible for its historical content that reveals how people lived back then, and it tells us to love all people and have no domination toward others. Thus, the ideas and spirit of the Bible is to <u>Love all others</u> and to <u>have no domination toward others</u> and all else in the Bible should be considered false.

But human pride causes "born again Christians" to think YOU must believe in their god, bible and go to their church to get to Heaven. The Jew and the Islamic think this too, but most of them do not push their beliefs unto others as the Christians do.

Then David came along, one of the many of today who declares that the Angels of God still talks to people, and he says, God's Angels have told him, "All religions belong to God. For everything and everyone is His, too. It does not matter what church you go to. It does not matter if you go to church at all. And do not place your false god beside or above Him. Live with Love in your heart for all. Have no domination toward others. For there is one Supreme One above all and He is GOD."

There can be many Houses of Jacob, and there can be many churches for God. God chooses as many and with as many names as He wishes to place upon His houses. Same as He can chose as many people to be His Prophets as He wishes to have. My human pride will not go against anything that He desires.

Do not let foolish human pride drag you into Hell. Except everything around you as being part of God. Except all religions as being of God. Allow all others to live in freedom as long as they and their actions do not impose upon others. Refuse all thoughts and concepts of domination to yourself and others, for they are of evil.

David has been away from *Jesus'* House of Jacob for a few days and yesterday when he returned he was told that a man e-mailed him and demanded that he remove from his Archive pages, one page from his Messages. He stated that David stole a Bible passage from him, and he claims that the House of Jacob that he attends is the true and only "church" of Jesus, so he pretty well accused David of lying about this being Jesus' House of Jacob.

First of all, David thought the Bible was written for all people, so how can one steal Bible passages from it?

Secondly, Jesus can have all the Houses and/or Churches that he chooses. David will not attempt to dictate to Jesus, God or anyone what he or she must or must not do.

But the human pride of this foolish man caused him to place his demands upon David. His stupid human pride makes him think everyone in the world will know that it is he that I wrote about.

Rather he knows it or not, David's web site was read around the world. He received e-mails daily from people seeking help or whatever, that live in many different places around the world. And this guy thinks he is so well known that everyone will know who he is. He is no better or worse than any of us, therefore he is not special, he is one of the billions.

Well let me tell you, people's human pride makes us feel special and people do not care who he is.

And this guy claims to be a Christian. I wonder if all Christians are like that?

God's Angels have instructed David to follow his heart. (They have not told me to remove the page, though he would not deny what God's Angels ask of me.)

Last week, Monday, the 15th of January, was celebrated as Martin Luther King Jr. day, a great man whose ancestry came out of slavery. Enough is being said about the man, I want to talk about Slavery.

Slavery, as of a defeated enemy, has been around since the dawn of time. After a war or battle the loser would became the slave to the victor. But we are not talking about that kind of slavery, we are talking about the black (African) slavery.

Why did the African become slaves around the world?

Who enslaved the Africans?

Around the 16th century the Europeans of the Catholic Church decided to spread its religion around the world. Once they entered the Americas and Africa, they realized that the natives of these places were very primitive compared to them.

Obtaining slaves from battles and wars were different; the losers in wars and battles could be as smart as the winners of the conflicts but just lost because of strategy. The natives of the Americas and Africa were like animals to the Europeans. So the Europeans quickly enslaved them.

One European who went to the Americas and thought that these natives were different - more intelligent than the African slaves. He campaigned to use and send only Africans as slaves in the other colonies and back to Europe.

Thus the black African slavery market began. For somewhere around 300 years black Africans were shipped to Europe, the Americas and else where in the world as slaves. Most Christians believed it was okay to own other people. The Christians that condoned slavery of those days felt they were living in a modern world as we do today. They placed things into their Bibles that said slavery was okay, then they removed things from their Bibles that forbid slavery.

What are the things that we placed in our Bible today says that our life styles of today are okay?

What have we removed from our Bible that forbid us from doing the wrong and sinful things that we do today?

Are we truly *"wiser"* than our forefathers?

Are we truly *"better"* than our brothers?

Does being Christian make a person closer to God than any other religion?

Is Christianity the only Religion of God?

Did not the people who lived during the 16th century think that during the mid 19th century, we could not own slaves, and also believe that they were not saved?

Were they not *Born Again* Christians back then?

Did they not pray to God for forgiveness of their sins?

Is it not once that you pray for forgiveness you are not to do the same sin again?

Once they prayed and asked for forgiveness for their sin, did they not own slaves anymore?

Did they release them?

Are not the people who were once enslaved trying to place domination on the other people of United States of America today?

Should not today the black race forgive the white race for our forefathers placing their forefathers into slavery?

It was not you or I that enslaved the Africans, it was our forefathers. We do not owe the black Americans anything.

When "Fair-a-con" had his million man march on Washington, where were the women?

(You see I spelled his name as he is.)

The Islamic Religion says, "Muhammad, the Son of God will be born to man and women will once again be a beast of burden."

'Fair-a-con" is once again trying to place blacks into slavery. Black men are placing their own women into slavery because of a religion and one of its leaders.

And David states, there is a young woman in the Marines who is stationed in Yuma, Arizona. Her name he will not mention. For weeks we then had been E-mailing each other as she asked him questions about the true God, the God of Abraham. As I answered her questions, she would give him her answer to her own question, her answers were false, lies from her. Today she E-mailed him and wrote, "Oh, I was just playing."

One does not "play" with questions about God. She and the church that she attends, I will not name her church but it is No-thing to God, but is still an Antichrist to humans. They - she and her church are Oblivious to God. They worship a false and pagan god who they named "jesus." They "feed" on our children who have joined the military, who are lost and stationed in Yuma. David speaks to her now, "Heed my words, you and those who attend and follow your church are doomed into the pits of Hell forever unless you disband. For you and your church are delivering God's children into slavery of your church and false god."

Islam Religion places people in slavery of its man made god - Muhammad. Muhammad was a person who once lived around 600 AD that the Muslims say is God or the Son of God. Hebrew Religion followed the true God - the God of Abraham, but places people in slavery because they lost Him with their denial of Jesus. Christianity places people into slavery because they place Jesus above God and worship Him instead of the true God. All three Religions use the Old Testament as the foundation of their Religion. Yet none of them can see that their Gods are the same One - the God that Abraham, Isaac and Jacob worshipped. Man has polluted and corrupted all the Religions that God helped them start. If and when the people would wake up and realize that their Gods are the same One but their Religions are different, there would be no more slavery or wars, then we could all live in peace with Love for all others.

"In the beginning there was Love, and Love was with God, and Love was God."

There are many things in this world that could place you in Hell, and there is no one but you that will know what is right for you. You be the judge for your life.

God did not intend for any of His children to be placed into slavery. Man places others into slavery for his own desires. Are we all not children of God?

Think outside of life because there are many ways that place you in Hell.

And David Prayed:

"My Lord, the True and Righteous Holy God above all, your children have not yet learned. I know only a few will be saved and most from all religions will be lost. Thank You for allowing me to help show and teach them Your Way. In the name of the true God of Abraham, Isaac and Jacob I pray. Amen."

Hell

There is not a place known as or called Hell on the Other Side. God created the concept of evil and Hell, man has created the actions of evil – Hell. Hells are made here on earth and created in the minds of humans.

There has been those who encountered NDEs, and claimed they have seen or visisted Hell, but the Hells are always as they think Hell would be. And these people may be being told that if they do not change the directions of their lives, this is where they are going after life.

Many people of today, will tell you they have ventured to the Other Side and have seen Hell when they were there. But they are merely seeing what they consider to be Hell after life.

The Soul of people that lived in Hell or had the actions of Hell during their life time, will remove themselves from the congregation of Angels after its death. And that will be its Judgment Day.

Judgment Day occurs after death and when the deceased first enters into the Other Side. That is usually the first time that the deceased realizes that his life was driven by self-centered concepts. And he does not want to be part of the congregation of God's Angels. (He does not want the other Angels to re-live his life.)

Man has created a place called Hell for control over his congregation. On the Other Side, Hell is not a place, it is the experiences of the life the deceased lived. One who lived life in Hell, may travel into the Light of the congregation of God's Angels and then realize he does not want to be with the Others and remove himself from their presence and roam on the Other Side forever, or he will destroy himself, and his destruction is his Judgment Day.

Hitler's Soul does not live in God's Heaven. He may have gone there, but he does not live there anymore or did not live there very long. Hitler's evil acts against other people came from him alone and what he did wrongly, places him in Hell. And he Judged himself and removed his Soul when he realized that he was wrong.

The Clergy that lied to the people, and did things against the children, and his life experiences are removed.

The people that thought and had sexual pleasure against others are not in Heaven.

An Angel may re-live the lives of those people that Hitler and others have killed. And that Angel will feel sad about what Hitler or the other killers did. The Angels would be able to re-live the lives and the deaths of all those who he killed. But the Angels will never re-live the lives of the killers.

The Angels will never feel the happiness or the pleasure that the killers felt. The lives of the killers, their self-centered feelings are gone forever from God and His Angels.

There are three levels of Sin;

1. Sin against the Spirit of Life. Saying and believing that there is nothing in God's Creation worth living for.
2. Sin against the Father. Saying and believing that another person has nothing to give to this Creration of God's.
3. Sin against the Father and Son. Saying or believing that another's religion is wrong.

These three Sins <u>may</u> be forgiven here on Earth, and <u>could</u> be forgiven in Heaven, but they are <u>Not</u> forgiven by God!

All three Sins contain suicide, killing of another or killing oneself or others Spiritually.

Do you remember the story of the "Onion Field Killing"?

Back in the 1960s, I believe, in the City of Los Angeles, two crooks kidnapped two policeman and drove them north toward Bakersfield. The crooks stopped in an onion field where they decided to kill the officers because back then, they would get the death penalty for kidnapping. They thought that by killing the officers, they could get away with it. They may have gotten away with it here on earth, but do you think that they got away with it with God?

Where do you think these guys are in God's Master Plan?

Today, many have decided that God forgives murderers, and they, the killers will live in Heaven forever, after they repent. WRONG!

God will not change His concepts because humans changed theirs.

(Oh by the way, the crooks did shoot and kill one of the police officers while the second officer got away.)

Directions to Heaven

Afterlife is your life experiences living forever within God's Congregation of Angels. The directions to Heaven may seem wide in human reality, but the gate to Heaven is narrow and not many will enter. It does not matter which religion one follows, it matters how that individual accepts God and His Creation into his life.

Salvation is the directions to Afterlife and Heaven, and Self-Salvation is the only way for you to get to Heaven.

When David was young, a saying went around about, "My brother can beat up your brother." The people say, "My God can beat up your God," and people are willing to die for their beliefs throughout time.

Theology schools only teaches what their professors have learned, they cannot think outside of the box of their religion. Humans can only think of God and the Other Side as life is here on earth. There is no Satan or Lucifer as Angels on the Other Side because all Angels in congregation are God. There is no rank in God – all are equal. Satan and Lucifer were created by humans for control over others. The evil acts toward others is true, but that is only the energy of the acts toward other people. And those evil acts toward others is chiseled into the Souls of many, and may place that Soul into denial. And those who on the Other Side that think as humans do, will not go to God's Heaven.

Judah follows the story of Moses, Christianity follows the beliefs in Jesus, Islam follows the beliefs of Muhammad, and all three beliefs were great, but the people who followed changed those beliefs into the concepts of man and destroyed God's understandings. The trash of religions need to be removed.

Today, people think as a child and not as an adult about death because people do not know how to teach their children about life, and they could not explain death to others; people believe death is an unpleasant topic and should not be discussed, but it is a position that all people will enter someday. The only thing is, who will die first?

When you claim you love another person, you should be able to remember what that person said, if that person said earlier what they would like to have, you should remember it at Christmas and buy it for them then. You should not worry about what to buy for them at Christmas time; we should remember all that they said throughout the year. That is love for that person, and we should remember what we said to another because that is love for yourself.

(Remember what you said and did, just as you should remember what they said and did also.)

The ones we love, we should remember them, and our actions relates back to loving God, and not only to the people that God or His Angels communicated with.

(Remember the concepts of all, including God.)

Love; is not only to others but also to ones self, and whereas, a promise to another is not only to them but is also to you.

Are we so busy that we cannot remember how our families and others feel?

Are we so busy we do not have time to remember God?

Did you ever pray to God and He did not answer?

Did He do you as you did to other people?

Do we as humans, expect God to treat us any differently than we treat others?

Can we expect the gates to Heaven to be opened for us, just because of who we are?

The children are the most blessed by God because they do not know hatred and follow only love. And those with love in their hearts are the most welcome into Heaven.

Relax and allow your heart to direct you toward God's Heaven. Love all others and have no domination toward them, and you will do fine.

You are not your brother's keeper; do not place him under your domination. Help those when you see help is needed.

You are your own banker; do not allow your church to take care of your money. Spread your money to those that need help.

Be the minister that God created and intended you to be. You have read of God's words in your Bibles, now inspire others to learn and know them.

The only direction to everlasting life with God is to treat all others as you wish to be treated, it does not matter which religion you follow. Who cares if you follow Moses, Jesus or Muhammad, they were only men that once lived. They, too, were God's, and are still His.

Heaven

The easiest way for me to explain Heaven is; Heaven is the Congreation of Angels that make up God. There is no building or place that is Heaven. Creation is the Heaven of everything.

Salvation is the directions that we travel in our time to either Heaven or Hell.

Many of those who have had NDEs, claim Heaven is a wonderful place as a garden setting. These people may well be told or believe that their lives have been good or consider their lives as good. But these peoeple talk of the continuation of life as it was here on earth. And more than likely, those people did not see Heaven but only their own views of their lives here on Earth.

Heaven is <u>NOT</u> a continuation of life nor is Heaven an extention of life. When life is over, the life style that you lived here on earth is over.

One of the biggest problems is people can only think in the concepts of this reality.

When David was young, he thought of Heaven as; living in a place as earth, he would visit with his parents at their home, and maybe go to the store and travel back to his home, day in and day out, just as he did here on earth.

David and I were talking one evening about Heaven and I told him that I wondered what people really thought that Heaven was.

I decided that I would start asking people to see what their concepts of Heaven were.

In speaking to one friend, who seemed to have a very loving and giving heart, I asked her what she thought Heaven was.

My friend told me that she thought that Heaven was a place that was very bright with a beautiful and tranquil light. She felt that their would just be an overwhelming feeling of peace and contentment filled with lots of love.

I thought that that was a pretty good answer. It made me want to find more people to ask. I thought that maybe people were beginning to realize that the traditional theory of Heaven was just that. A theory!

So, I called another friend.

This friend wasn't sure how to answer. She said that she wasn't sure, but she felt that Heaven would be a place where there was a feeling of lots of love. When asked what she thought it would look like, once again she said she wasn't sure, but she thought it would be like a beautiful garden, but not like what we know here. This garden would flourish with very bright colors and there would be a brilliant light that would shine throughout. Then she told me that it was really difficult to put into words what she actually was picturing in her mind.

Once again, I thought that it wasn't a bad answer.

So, I called another friend.

This friend I knew, unlike the other two friends, was committed to a certain church, although I did not know which church he belonged to. When I asked him what he thought Heaven would look like, he told me he had no idea. I asked him how he could have no idea and he told me that he never really thought about it. This absolutely floored me. How could this guy be so involved in his church and not have some idea about Heaven. So then I asked him what his church thought Heaven was and that surely his minister has talked about Heaven and Salvation. My friend told me no that they never really talk about it. I said okay then asked him to just think about it for a minute and tell me what he thought. He told me he just had no idea. What really disturbed me was that he didn't seem to even care about it.

My next call was to a minister friend of ours.

I told him about the people I had asked what they thought Heaven was like and what their responses were. He was so aghasted with the answers I received that he never really said what he thought Heaven was. He did tell me that he thought there would be an unbelievable brilliance of light.

After life, on the Other Side, is in the concepts of God and His Congregation, that does not fit into reality here on earth.

You, your Soul– God's Angels will be able to see the individuals of your life as you saw those people in life. If that person was young when you died, then you will see that person at the age that you knew him when he was alive. You are only reviewing your life that you once lived and your life ended when that person was young. But if you would review that person's life from his side of life, then you would review all that he did in life after your demise, and then, you could see him at the age he was when he died, his complete life.

As the Angel that lived your life, walks into the congregation of God's Angels, He may re-live your life; all that you did in your life.

And He would be able to travel into the future and see things that happened after your demise. That Angel or other Angels may say, "Wow, I want to see more of this life, but from different directions."

The Angel then re-lives the lives of your friends to understand how they re-acted to your actions. The Angel then could re-live all of the Christmas' or other special days that you experienced but from the different directions of all that were around you during your life.

The Angel may re-live the lives of those who ever knew you; the Angels could re-live and be able to feel how those people loved you, and how they felt with their feelings of loving you.

As for those that held hatred in their heart toward you, their lives are not there for others to re-live, but their feelings against you will remain in the hearts of others (God's Angels) as They, the Angels, experienced their feelings toward you, but not the feelings of the evil ones.

If they had bad feelings toward others, the Angel would only be able to see and feel how others felt toward them, but those with bad recorded experiences (Soul) will not be there, only those things of what they did and how others felt about them will be there for the Angels to review. The evil lives experiences will not be there for others to relive or experience.

(The pleasures felt by them doing bad things to others will be gone.)

If a person killed another, no Angel will be able to re-live the killings of another. They will not be able to expereince how the other felt when killing another human. The feelings of killing will be gone, and in accordance, all evil actions (pleasures) displayed against any other living thing will be gone; the evil life will be removed from God's Angels.

If your ancestors had an acceptable life, an Angel may go back into the past and re-live the lives of those ancestors. The Angel would be able to feel what they felt toward others back then. In other words, the Angel would be able to re-live (see and feel) how your great-grandfather felt about your great-grandmother, and re-live all that they did while alive.

If your life was not for and part of God, then an Angel could only be able to experience all those who (with God in their hearts) were connected to you.

If God is accepted into your life and one of God's Angels stands by you throughout your life – the Angel with-in, your recorded experiences (your life) will remain with God. Then, any of God's Angels would be able to re-live your life as that Angel experiences (re-lives) your life.

Again, you cannot examine a single strand of life to know the life's complete picture, you must examine the complete ball of string to understand all the things that made up that indiviual's life.

We should not judge a person until we understand his complete life because we could never understand everything in his life. Therefore, we should only judge his actions to see if his actions are correct for us.

Once, David asked the Angel Jo, "Could I go to see Heaven?"

She answered, "Yes, you could, but you should not leave your body for any length of time because if you are gone for very long, your body would start to die."

So, David did go into Heaven for a short time in human time, but time is continual on the Other Side. As David walked into God's Heaven, he was greeted by a few old friends. They enjoyed each others lives as they enjoyed his, too.

(Any Angel of God may go back into the time of your life and re-live part or all of your life as many times as He wishes.)

After David went back into his body, the Angel Jo and he talked again. And the Angel Jo said unto David, "Life was not designed to be prefect. Life was made to experience. Just as Jesus once told the people that He did not come to bring peace but instead to bring conflict into the world.

"All lives are innerwoven, all that you do effects others and all that others do, in some way, effects you. It is not your concern what others think about you, it is your concern what you say, think and how you act to others and yet, it is okay to dislike the actions of others, but do not hate them. Hatred grows into evil, and that will place your thoughts into Hell.

"You will not fully understand all that We say until you join Us on this the Other Side, but you should try to hear and follow what We say for We mean only the best for you. We love not only you but all who live.

"We understand that humans only know life as that in which they live, and yet, We try to show and teach them of God's Love. But most cannot comprehend life until after death, though We continue to direct Our Love toward them for it is their choice to receive it and return God's Divine Love or not, for We will not dominate you or them.

"Many on this Side, that which you call the Other Side, call you the Guider for you guide others toward God. It does not matter which religion they prefer because all religions belong to the one God at the top, as long as their religion says to love all people and have no domination toward others, they will do fine. And yet, if they would just lift their Souls - feel free, live free, touch free, love free and above all else, be free, then We would rejoice and sing with them.

"If people would only realize that they are part of the human race and that part of God resides in them as the Angel-within them, and treat others as they wish to be treated and as they should treat themselves, all would be fine. For those who lived a righteous life without the need to have heard or seen are the most rewarded in the Light."

And David prayed, "Father, thank You for giving me the guidance of Jesus and Your Angels. Amen."

And the Angel Jo continued, "Confession of Sin does not remove the Sin unless the Sin does not occur again.

"Asking the Father for forgiveness of a Sin does not receive Forgiveness unless the Sin does not occur again.

"One must be able to self-judge in order to repent from one's past thoughts, ideas and concepts. One should know the difference between right and wrong actions they reflect upon others, in order to self-judge. The knowledge of right and wrong comes with maturity - growth.

"This self-judgment is not only for a spiritual level, but for all things that are involved in your daily life.

"The Father will not hold it against you if you happen to carelessly repeat the Sin, but you should try not to repeat the Sin, for if you repeat the Sin, you have forgotten God. But God does not forget you, for you live in His heart as He should live in yours.

"People think of Sin that which is only against God, but all things against the Father, the Son or Holy Ghost, these are Spirits of Sins. The Father, Son and Holy Ghost are all things in life and including all life. Whenever you do anything against another or against human society or man-made laws, you have committed a Sin, for that act is against life as God has intended life to be, and against the things that lifted you from animal.

"Those who repeatedly confess about committing the same Sin shall not be forgiven; those who repeatedly ask forgiveness for the same Sin shall not receive Forgiveness.

'For if one admits to committing a Sin, then he knows the difference between right and wrong. And those who knowingly do wrong are of the dog and not of God.

"The Father is very loving to His children and does allow them to lie to themselves, but He is very demanding and will not allow them to lie to Him when they try to enter His Kingdom."

And the Angel Jo faded away, and Jesus stood in Her place, and He said unto David, "Do not fear, for you shall not be judged for other's actions against humanity. For when the time comes, God - that part of God within each that you refer to as the Angel-within, shall judge the life that He has lived. The Gate to Heaven is narrow and not many will enter, less than one of one percent of one percent shall be saved, and those saved shall come from all religions and all time. Even most who claim to be Christians - the ones who say they follow Me do not and they shall not be saved either. Proclaiming repentance in confession or asking for forgiveness will not save them unless they truly change. We have given each their individual choice to Heaven and most have refused Us. You as well as all others shall be judged for only what each individual has done. Enjoy life and raise your Soul, find the Salvation that you need and allow others to follow theirs.

'Presently there is fighting between Christians and Muslims in Indonesian Borneo. In Yogoslavia there was fighting between

Muslims and Christians. There was fighting between Muslims and Buddhist people in Afghanistan, and the Muslims are fighting the Jews in Israel. And on a Monday the 5th of March, it was reported that 35 Muslims were crushed to death during the Islamic Hajj. Did you think these people will ever be saved or in Heaven?"

It seems to David that the Muslims have demonstrated their Satanic agressive nature not only toward their own people with their senseless religious rights, but also toward people of different religions ever since Muhammad first started his cult that we call Islam. If we allow the Muslims to overtake Isreal, they will not stop until Islam governs the world.

David said, "Live with Love for all others and to try not to dominate others."

But he is not against using force to stop another from placing others under their domination. A Love for a Love or a slap for a slap.

God's Angels communicated with Moses and started the Jewish Religion. Jesus lived and from his teachings of Love came Christianity. And it is said that God's Angels communicated with Muhammad and he started Islam and converted people by the sword to his religion. Yet, Christianity and Islam both refer back and use the Old Testament as part of their religious writings while the Hebrew Religion refers to the Old Testament as their Torah. Did you think those who place their religion above the true God will be saved?

And the Angel Jo again stood where Jesus just stood, and She said unto David, "Until you arrived to this, the Other Side, you could not fully understand God's Master Plan.

"You do not understand why God allowed the Islamic Religion to start in the first place for it is against all people. But His Plan of life contained Islam. You must know by following what is in your heart that you are doing what will be done as God's Will.

"But if Muslims or any other attempts to injure or control people by terrorist attacks, throwing fire bottles and rocks at people because of their religion, they should be put down as the dogs they are. For Muslims were given the opportunity to live in peace with the other people on earth, but they refused and want the world for their own. Their Heaven is only Hell.

"Soon you will see a calm of three days in Israel then war in Israel will break out as never seen before. After this battle, the Hebrew Nation will stand again in size that is was during the days of its greatness of the Old Testament."

To the true God of Abraham, Isaac and Jacob, David prayed:

"My Lord, the True and Righteous Holy God above all, forgive us for what must be delivered unto the evil ones on this world. The Earth was placed here by You and we were created by You to experience and enjoy, yet others try to dominate and demand us to bow down to their god and not to Worship him. Those with Satanic ideas and beliefs, who try to dominate us must be removed. Destroy those who refuse You. The time has come for You to bring peace to the land of Israel as prophesied by John in the Book of Revelation as Israel expands back to its original size that it once was.

"Thank You for another day and for all that You have given me to use during this life. Help me rise above the dog with the knowledge of You. Guide me to Your Kingdom and everlasting Love. I try to hold You in my heart constantly and control the dog, but if and when I fail, please forgive me as I repent. Amen."

And the Angel Jo continued and said unto David, "Your mission of writing our books is over. Yes, you may start a 'Church' but not many will come. They will not understand what you say, the others to come after you will explain our words to them. For you have layed the foundation and only time is needed now. Enjoy and experience life as you continue to help others on both Sides as Heaven awaits you.

"Most of the world could use your guidance, if they would listen but they won't. The ones who seek help and come to you for such, may find their Salvation to Everlasting Life, but also, there are others in the world who are the same as you. We use as many as necessary, but do you not think that they also enjoy and experience life?

"Your help to others that I speak of is the Inspiration that you were given to help others to seek God and the religion that fits their needs. Let them see the life style that you now demonstrate, let your life style be the inspiration they seek. Live with an open heart to all and have no domination toward others, then they too shall seek God. That is what We have done with you.

"You have many things to enjoy and experience before you once again return Home, but you also, have many to inspire for you are not only a Master but also the servant.

"Blessed are those who not only lead but follow, too."

Then, she was gone.

And David prayed, "God, thank You for allowing us another day. Please forgive us for what we have done, we did not understand but we are learning. Continue to guide us in our daily lives, and help us to move toward what You expect of us. Amen."

In the early hours before morning, David was awaken by a bright light in our bedroom as he turned over toward the light, he saw a person whom he had never met but knew him to be the Angel Michael. He stood about 5 feet 8 inches tall and appeared to be very muscular and was wearing some kind of soldiers uniform as if from the ancient Greek or Roman era and simlar to what the Angel Gabrael wears. The Angel Micheal also drifted like smoke and his face seemed blurred, too.

The Angel Micheal said unto David, "Yes it is I, Micheal, the one believed to be God's Warrior and yet, I am also a Guardian as with all of Angels of God's. And for now, I am the Guardian of your youngest son. I will guard, protect and guide him as others have done so in the past and as We try to do with all people in the world. Yet, the people in the world who are of the world refuse our help, they do not have eyes to see us with or ears to hear us with for they have been taught to believe only what others tell them.

"People believe Me to be God's Warrior because they have been taught there is rank in Heaven, but in Heaven is the peace within one's self and all are equal in God for all are part of God. And people in the world who are of the world use rank in their religions to hold domination over others.

"Fear not, for I will take care of your son as God has promised to guard, protect and guide you and your family. Non-believers words will not harm you nor will their stones touch you or your family. We shall stand beside you forever. For you have followed God's request - You have layed the foundation for Jesus' House of Jacob - the Son's House of Jacob, for you are David but the Angel-within you is Jacob. Therefore, your body is a House of God - the Father and the Son's House, as should be with all people.

"The Angel Jacob that dwells within you may not be the Jacob indicated in the Christian Bible but it is irrelevant to you who He is, for the Christian religion, too, has been twisted by domination toward others and much of the Truth cannot be found there.

"Blessed are the ones who truly believe and follow the Father and the Son. And yet, do not tempt God but follow the Angel-within with Love for all and no domination toward others. For the Angel-within you is part of God as with all others."

Then the Angel Micheal was gone.

To the Father - the true God of Abraham, Isaac and Jacob, David prayed:

"My Lord, the True and Righteous Holy God above all, thank you for another day and all that you have allowed us during this day. Forgive me of my sin and help me understand them so that I will not make them again tomorrow. Thank you for letting your Angels help and guide my family and me. Amen."

As David lay there, he remembered that when he was in Heaven, he saw Jesus standing in a place and Jesus held a stick in His left hand and drew in the dirt with the stick as He squatted on the ground and talked to others that sat and squatted in front of Him while listening to His words of wisdom. In the distant past soon an angry mob approached Jesus from the village behind Him. As they came near, a man in the mob said. "Rabbi, we have found this woman as a prostitute. Shall we stone her as it is written in the Torah?"

Jesus did not lift his head toward the people but instead kept drawing in the dirt near His feet. Silently all stood still while they waited for His answer.

Within a few minutes Jesus answered, "If there is one among you that has not sinned, let him cast the first stone."

He continued to play in the dirt, the people in the mob looked at each other, dropped their stones they held in their hands and left the prostitute there and quitely walked back toward the village.

Still without looking up Jesus continued to draw in the dirt and said to the prostitute, "Go your way but do not do that again."

The woman left and never was a prostitute again.

Without teaching or preaching (bitching) to the prostitue, Jesus caused her to change her life style.

And then David saw in the past of 1996, when the Angel Joleen entered into his life, he found another Angel hanging around. The Angel Joleen did not tell him the name of this other Angel, she waited until he asked Her His name. Then She answered, "Oh, that's Gab, He is just a friend of ours who comes by to visit now and then."

(It was at that time of the past, David did not know who Gabrael was.)

Afterwards, David started reading the Christian Bible and found out who Garbael was. And then he remembered, he accepted Him being around the Angel Joleen, and he learned much from Him in the years that followed.

Then David remembered another Angel started appearing and he asked his son to ask him who He was, his son replied, "He is the Helper."

(That was when David first saw the Helper and asked Him what His name was, He answered, "Jesus." For his son, Daniel and he did not know the Helper was the Son of God - Jesus.)

In the past of re-living David's life, he saw the Angel Joleen turning his life around but not forcing a different life style upon him. She was inspiring him to change his life style. For when he was ready to ask, She was ready to answer his questions.

In today's reality of society, we try to teach our children how to live, yet we are inspiring them to steal, lie and kill.

We as humans need to inspire others (that includes our children) to learn about God and to have better life styles. We cannot and should not force our life style, religion or beliefs upon others. For forcing something upon another is domination and that is the root to all sins.

It is wrong to force your religion unto others. It is wrong to force others to listen to how you were saved because Salvation is individualized.

The starving person will vomit if at first you feed them too much. One must wait for the hungry to ask before offering them God. That is exactlly what Jesus did with the prostitute and that is exactlly what the Angel Jo did with David - when they were ready for change, They helped them change.

Inspire others so that they want to listen to what you say about God. Inspire others to want to know more about the God that you talk about. Inspire others to change their life styles. But only talk of God and your religion when someone ask you about them.

To the true God of Abraham, Isaac and Jacob, David prayed:

"My Lord, the True and Righteous Holy God above all, forgive us for our sins and grant us the intelligence to inspire others. Give us the patience and wisdom to help others improve themselves as we, too, improve ourselves. Dear Father, thank You for granting me the insight to the wonderful things that Your Angels have inspired me with the knowledge to understand as I learn more about You and Your ways. Amen."

Late during an evening on or around the fifth of February in the year of 2000, as the Angel Jo and David were having a conversation, in which they discussed his future and his starting of *Jesus'* House of Jacob, Jesus appeared and floated across the room and stopped in front of David at the foot of the bed, while Jo sat on the edge of his bed and David in a chair beside its headboard.

Jesus said, "Can you see Me?"

David answered, "Yes, but You look very faint."

Jesus replied, "Turn off the light so you can see Me better."

David turned off the light and could see Him clearer as He floated about two feet off the floor, therefore, it was difficult for David to judge His height. He wore some kind of white robe, His hair was thick as if it was curly and dark in color that did not seem to go to His shoulders but David could not determine its length for His total shape glowed and appeared as smoke.

Jesus continued, "I cannot tell you if your life will end today, tomorrow, next week, next year or two years from now, but your mission is not over yet. You will help others but you are not the one who will speak the words that We have given you."

"But," David interrupted, "My body is old and weak, and my body hurts and I cannot work anymore, how can I undertake building the foundation for your House. And the world is not like it was long ago, today we must have money to live. What do I do when bill collectors start calling and beating on my door?"

Jesus answered, "My Brother, Our children of the world need your help. Yes, they are your children also for we are all One. You must tell them as I did. Tell them of your pains and hurts as I once told them of My pains and of My hurts. Bring them together. They will come and listen to you. They will believe in what you say.

"When the blockage in your arteries occurred, We were there.

When you had the by-pass surgery, We were there. We have been beside you throughout your life, We will always be beside you. We will guard and protect you and take care of you and your family, my brother.

"Follow your heart with NEVERTHELESS but expect and accept whatsoever that you sow. When you give help, friendship and love expect them to be learned and given out by the ones who you gave them to. If others who received your help, friendship and love do not pass them on, refuse them for they do not want to learn. But if someday they change, then open your heart to them. For if a person was once bad and is now good, open your heart to them and do not judge them for their past mistakes. And if a person was once good and is now bad, try to help them change but if they do not change, close your heart to them, for then you are placing yourself in Self-domination. But remain where you are for someday they may change. And yet, mourn seven days for the dead, and cry for the dead in the world."

And the Angel Jo said, "Remember My touch and I am there beside you. And the night before your death, I shall appear and tell you, and the next day, you will be busy helping others and forget about what is coming. When you pass over to this, the Other Side I will be there to hold and comfort you."

And Jesus added, "When your time comes, the world will be sadden, but here We will rejoice at your Home coming. But for now follow your heart. Blessed are those who truly understand God's ways and follow His desires without self-reservations. Until we meet again, my brother, I Love you."

David responded, "I love you too, my brother."

And then, They were gone.

To the true God of Abraham, Isaac and Jacob, David prayed:

"My Lord, the True and Righteous Holy God above all, thank you for allowing me this life to experience and enjoy. Forgive us for our sins and give us the knowledge to know what our sins were. Grant us the intelligence to understand the truth so we do not commit the same sin again. Guide and protect us as we travel through this life and bless those who Love You. Amen."

Since David talks with God's Angels, he can comprehend how

people who have never communicated with God or His Angels directly would think what is written into the Bible as true. But God did not write the Bible, He merely spoke to others who in turn wrote the Bible, therefore, the Bible is full of pollution from its writers.

Read your Bible to understand that it speaks of "Live with Love from an Open Heart for All" throughout its pages and anything other than that is from man!

Remember that we are human and all humans can and do make mistakes (things that are not on target) for the word "sin" means "not on target," and God does not make mistakes! The word "sin" means making mistakes is anything that you do wrong, not hitting the target, not doing things or not living correctly.

To the true God of Abraham, Isaac and Jacob, David prayed:

"My Lord, the True and Righteous Holy God above all, thank you for allowing us another day to experience life. Forgive us for our sins and guide us into the direction to know what our sins were. Grant us the intelligence to understand the truth so we do not commit the same sin again., forgive us, your children for what we have done and teach your children about your concept of life. Guide us into the correct way to live. Show us the way to Love. Guide us, the foolish ones, help us see our mistakes. Turn our selfishness toward Love for all others. Help us to remove our sin of self-center feelings and re-place it with understanding of life. Forgive those who have fallen before us.

"My Lord, forgive me as I forgive all others and myself who have sinned against me. Help all of us make the right choices in life. Guide us in Your intended direction of life. I mourn for the dead, yet I still cry for the dead that are still alive. Please deliver them from their evils that dwell within themselves. Once again confirm to the Christians that Jesus is not God, but is Your Son. Guide the foolish ones, help them see their mistakes. Turn the eyes of the sinner from inward to outward. Direct the shepherd to teach instead of consuming his flock. Lead not us to better pastures but to guide the pastors to better understanding of Your Love. Help me understand and to forgive those who do not accept You for what You are as You have forgiven those who refuse You. Forgive me of my sins that I have committed today. Guide me to learn not to make those same mistakes again. Help me forgive those who have sinned against me today. Direct me in Your Righteous way to live. Thank You for allowing me another day and may you also grant me another day tomorrow. Thank You for allowing Your Angels to enter my life and guide me. Amen."

As David remembers seeing in Heaven, President Bush spoke to the people of the world in is his address to the Congress, "If you are not with us, then, you are with the terrorist."

Thus, he has divided the world into two; one fighting against terrorism and the other group is the terrorist - a world divided into two parts, fighting against each other - World War Three. But the life that he once lived was not there for David to enter.

And the Angel Jo said unto David, "All have individual rights, now we shall see if their choices to fight terrorist is the same as their war against drugs or do they truly mean a war against terrorist. We know the answer, but now they shall experience their answer. The people shall learn and experience through their actions and endure them no matter what the outcome may be. God has given all the gift of individual choices, the teachings throughout their lives, taught by others shall govern their choices and decisions. Will the dog or Angel within win?

"What does Revelations say?

"Could Revelations be wrong?

"Did man or God write it?"

And David replied to the Angel Jo, "If they, the people cannot understand or hear what You have said through me and others, that is their displeasure and not my concern. You nor I can demand God upon others. The Love of God flows through many including me but the dead shall never hear or feel Him, they shall forever drift in their Hells until the end of time. I shall not Judge their Hells but only feel sadness for their actions that they place upon others and themselves, for I control only my dog. I wish that the people of the world were different and that Revelations was wrongly written, but I, too, know the answers to your questions. I hold God's Will in the highest respect, I will not reveal the date of the end. And I know that many things written into Revelations were the thoughts, ideas and concepts of man, but the Spirit of it is true. Therefore, the ending of time may not come or be as it is written, but an end shall come as prophesized. I know that time only means something to humans, therefore, the Third World War could and may last for years, maybe even hundreds of years, but this war is not the end, for other things must pass before the end comes. I understand that all that I have learned was taught to me for my Salvation, and were given to me symbolically for my understanding, and many do not understand what I have passed on to them."

Then Jesus stood where the Angel Jo once stood and said to David, "We Inspire people to seek God in their own devise, thus, we teach Salvation to them. I am only one, but one who is held high in God, and yet, all as individuals are held high in God, for all are His Children and all are equal. Therefore, all others, you and I are not only the Master but also the servant. Allow your heart - God's Love to cry out to the dead to seek God, but do not allow your weeping to control you nor force God upon them. Each will experience as it is written in the Master Plan, for when the job is ready for them, they will be ready for the job."

David replied to Jesus, "Yes, my Brother, I shall keep God in my heart and for those who seek Him as I experience life."

And then the Angel Gabrael stood in the place of Jesus and said to David, "God instructed Us to teach you, and you have learned, now you are ready for the job ahead of you."

David replied to the Angel Gabrael, "Your teachings from God shall guide me."

And then the Angel Jo re-appeared again and said to David, "The war must endure but taking of a life is not the answer, but they must learn at their own pace. You have learned, teach of Love... violence shall not come from you or to you, but remember, 'A love for a love as the same as a slap for a slap.' We, as promised, shall stand beside you and guide you, and protect and take care of you and your family forever."

Then, the word, "AMEN," echoed through the skies as the warmth of God's Love flowed down over me.

And the Angel Joleen continued and said unto David, "Do not brood over the wisdom of the world. For wisdom and intelligence are fulfilled at the level desired and needed by the individual for all are born equal. The need and desire to learn are inspiration that one seeks in his life. You cannot inspire those that do not wish inspiration nor can you push learning onto them for pushing knowledge onto others is domination and that we will have no part of. Your world is presently full of people pushing their concepts of their man made god and ideas about God onto others. You are to speak with Love in your heart for all. You are to have no domination toward others. The things that We instructed you to write along with your life style that you now demonstrate, will have impact on some. The Love that you show will inspire others to follow God's way of life - Love for all and no domination toward others.

"There is a certain man that you know of, he once had high expectations of life and was working very hard to achieve them but now he has lost his way because of his marriage to a certain woman and their expected unborn child. You nor I nor God will change what will come in his life for he has the final decision of his choices and yet, his wife has pulled him down to her level of wisdom and that is wrong for he should have inspired her to climb in intelligence. He should have guided her to Heaven in her thoughts but instead she has lead him into her Hell.

"God does not call for or ask for wars, murder or suicide of His children. For those things are of the dog. Teach as to inspire others not to make war, to kill or to commit suicide in the name of God or for God. And yet, tell them to protect themselves and fight if needed to preserve their individual rights of choice.

"All people have individual choices in life and their choices may not be the same as yours for their wisdom and intelligence may not be the same as yours and they may not have the same priorities as you, therefore love them for who they are - a human that contains an Angel within. But you need not love their actions for they may be different than yours.

"The certain young man and his wife that I spoke about, you cannot prophesize with accuracy if their unborn child will live or not or what their lives will bring for only God knows that. Love them but you may be sadden at their decisions that they have made as one. For they will someday stand in front of God to be judged as one for their actions during the time they spent together.

"And yet, this certain couple are only two of the billions of the world that do not have the wisdom or intelligence to know or understand God, let alone life. And their actions are not your problem or concern, for you are to enjoy and experience life as they also should do.

"Repent of your past actions of unkindness toward others - Forgive yourself as you ask God to forgive you of these past sins, but do not make the same mistake twice. Climb higher with wisdom of life as you learn as inspired by God's Concept of Life - *To Learn and Experience through the Experiences of Others through Endurance of Life.*

"Blessed are you who faithfully follow the Father and Son with wisdom in your hearts that show Love for all and no domination toward others. We shall forever guide and protect you for We love you, too."

And David prayed:

"Dear God, thank You for allowing your Angels to inspire me into seeking You. And thank You for all that You have given me, including this day. Forgive me when I become confused and strengthen me whenever others try to pull me down into their Hells for my dog thoughts or words. I will try to leash the dog, but sometimes he will get loose, in those times, I will remember Your touch to remove the dog's control. I know what I do is not for my ego but for Your Glory. I know not many will come to me, but those who do, shall be inspired by Your words that I speak to them, and some shall carry Your words to the world. I shall do as You have inspired. Amen."

Life Left Behind

The body decays back into that in which it came from. The Soul is the recorded experiences of the life of the body and that is what will remain.

And those, recorded experiences of the body, is the Engery of life that should live forever, if the human allows it. But that depends upon the individual and his actions. There are negative and/or positive Energy of the life of the person (Soul) who just past on to the Other Side.

In the early 80s, we had a friend who was dying from lung cancer, and his biggest fear was that when he died a close friend of his would live with or marry his to be widowed wife. This friend of ours planned on killing his wife to keep his friend away from her, and asked David to bring him a knife when he was in jail for killing his wife. David recalled answering him, "Yes, I will."

David knew that he would not help his friend in murder or suicide, but "Peace of his mind, was worth the truth," so it was irrelevant to David what would happen to his friend's wife after his demise.

After our friend past on from lung cancer, his friend did play around with his widow, and many times David wondered why his friend did not come and do his wife's boy-friend in.

(This was our friend who called me from the Other Side, that you read about in our Chapter Entities.)

And then, David thought about my dad, Joey. He hated David so much, why didn't he come back to do him in?

And how about all the other people in the world that died and hated others so much that they would do anything, even live in Hell forever, to get even with them. Why did those people not come back to harm the living?

Why did Hitler not come back and finish the job that he started and wanted done – killing all the Jews and taking over the world?

When we see an Entity, we are seeing an Angel carrying the recorded experiences of the deceased – their Soul.

When life is over, your life is over, the individual's life does not continue afterwards. All that you experience will end when your life is over. All the earthly goods and all that you possess or do not possess are insufficient to Angels. And what happens to our belongings does not matter what will happen or what will occur to a Soul. Therefore, it does not matter what you own or did not own to the Soul or the Angel. Nor does it matter who marries or does not marry when you are dead, and it surely doesn't matter who will own your car or house; your Soul, is your life experiences that will stop when you die.

If your life experiences are positive, they will combine with the Congregation's experiences, and that is God.

If your experiences are negative, your experiences of life may linger on the Other Side, but they will not join the Congregation.

Negatives are No-thing to God – the Congregation.

Positives are the concepts that are for God – the Congregation of Energy.

Our Souls - the experiences of our lives should be for the Angels of God – the Congregation to re-live and experience.

When that Angel re-views our lives, we are then as if re-living our lives.

In life, on this Side, you may see Entities at different times of their lives. You may view the ghost of a deceased child happy that died a horrible death because you are seeing that child at a wonderful time in the life of that child. And on the other hand, you could see the ghost of that same child crying as he did before he died because then he is re-viewing the horrible death of the deceased child just moments before his death.

Angels re-view or re-live the minutes, hours or the daily lives of the individual Soul.

And while re-viewing the Soul's activity, the Angel looks like that person did in life. And that Angel can come back and look like an inanimate object or as an animal.

(You must remember that "Time" is like on a continual plane on the Other Side where the Angels can go to different times without living each second or minute as we do – time is for the living here on earth.)

During the spring of 2005, our oldest son, Tony, wanted to take his motorcycle back to North Carolina from our home in California, and asked David to ride across the country with him. On their trip, David got thinking back to the time when he was young and a friend, Jerry Middleton, took him to the Morrow County Fair in Ohio. Over the years, David had often thought of Mr. Middleton taking him to that fair, but he never told him 'thank you'. When they entered North Carolina, David decided that he would leave Tony and ride north, up to Wooster, Ohio, to tell Jerry Middleton 'thank you' for taking him to the Morrow County Fair back when he was young. When David arrived in Wooster, Ohio, he found Jerry and his wife, Mary, still living in the same house. Jerry was surprised to find that David rode across the country just to tell him 'thank you'. Jerry was now eighty years old and was happy that David remembered. That is a positive that they will cherish forever and should re-live after death.

The negative actions of our lives are not re-viewed as re-living those lives. And then those actions are forgotten - not worth re-living, No-thing to God, they are deleted from the thoughts of God's Angels. And that is the self-judgment that each person will live in the Last Day of Time as the Judgement Day of God. And with time being continual of the Other Side, that Judgement Day will come as soon as your demise occurs. When we die, we leave life behind; we will not ever experience the good or bad again.

Follow God

As we continue our journey through understanding *Beyond and After Life*, you must realize that many parts of the Judah religion came directly or indirectly from the religions of Egypt.

(Moses was an orphan who was raised by the Egyptians, and this would be where his relgious upbringing originated.)

The Egyptians where the first known people who followed a one God religion – Monotheism concepts. All three of the major religions today still follow that style of belief.

Jews were a passive people, who allow others to steal regilious ideas from their Torah. The Christians stole the Old Testament because their New Testament was not big enough or interesting enough to carry their new Religion without it.

The Muslims stole the Christian or the Torah concepts to prove Muhammad communicated with a high ranking Angel of God's, Gabrael.

(Old Testament of the Christian Bible was first recorded into history as part of the Hebrew Religion and then after Christianity, these things were written into the Islamic Religion. Thus, we are not just talking of life, for you are learning the true meanings of the Old Testament, that is contained into the three major religions of the world and with this, we are talking of the recorded history of the world.)

Monotheist claim that their God is the only God above all; Jews say to be a Jew, one must be a descendant of Adam and Eve. Christians claim you must be born again to their Savior - Jesus. Islam claims, once you convert to Islam you can never leave.

The big difference between the three religions are their thoughts about Heaven.

Judah does not have a Heaven in their beliefs.

Christians believe in Heaven and Hell.

Muslims claim those who have not followed Allah will go to Hell, but all Muslims will eventually go to Heaven.

But to understand any part of religion, first we must discuss one of the biggest questions ever conceived by man, "Who or what is God?"

No matter which religion you follow or believe in, you should believe in Ghosts and afterlife becasuse Ghosts are near us in our daily lives. And then, you must also believe there are good and bad Energy. Therefore, think of the name "God" as being plural for good Ghosts and Satan as plural for bad Energy. But there is no Satan or Devil because only bad energy exists. God created everything, even the bad. He would not allow evil to exist in His Reality, and He would not allow wars to be fought on Earth for His plane. In His Reality, there is nothing that is bad, all is beautiful in His Reality.

God can also be referred to as the "Miracle of Life," for He is the "thing" that gives mineral and matter that made up our bodies, its mobility and its ability to think - comprehension. But the ability to think does not make our bodies the house in which God dwells as all living things have that capability. The separation between other living things and humans is the ability that God has given humans to rationalize and that is our comprehension, and that is the true miracle of human life. Another word that you can use to describe God is the word "Energy." For when the body dies, the Energy does not leave, the body leaves as it decays back to that of which it came from – minerals and other matter that make up the the Universe and Earth and the human bodies.

Energy does not die, it may change its form and direction because Energy is constant and remains forever. The Energy that lives forever is the engery of your actions when you were in body on this world.

Think of the power that it takes to move a finger on your hand, a rock cannot move part of itself. And if you stand above a rock and prepare to hit it with a hammer, it cannot and does not think about what is going to happen to it. But if you stand above a person and prepare to hit him with a hammer that person can and will think about what is about to happen, and yet, both, the human and rock, are made up of similar material. The difference between the rock and the person is the Energy – God that dwells within that person and not in the rock. God has created all and this three-dimensional universe is where we live. This universe and all that is in it is symbolic as a concept of God's. We can only comprehend the physics that pertains to our universe. We cannot understand the complexity of God. For God does not live in this three-dimensional plane, but He has the ability to travel through and dwell inside whatever and whenever He wishes, and He has chosen the human body as His House. Therefore, I refer to that part of God that dwells within each of us as the Angel-within, for all Angels in congregation is God.

David once heard a person say, "God "IS" because He is the "I" of is and the "S" of "IS" for He is the first and the last parts of everything for He is ALL," and that pretty well puts it back to God owns everything, including us.

And as we stroll through the understanding of Life, keep in mind that the Old Testament was originally transcribed thousands of years ago by primitive and ignorant people based on their knowledge of that day. This is the similar way the people of tomorrow will feel about this present time and us. For those people who lived the stories in the Old Testament could only describe the events in words of their language of that day. Therefore, many things written into the Old Testament and New Testament could easily be said and described more accurately today, but shall even be better described tomorrow.

To better understand how time plays a big part in descriptive words used in text, look at the understanding, concepts and thinking of hard-line Muslims of today. Their reality comes directly from the 700s, in which Muhammad lived, who claimed people must live as he did back when the Old Testament and new Testament was written.

Also, keep in mind that those who lived the stories of the Bible used scribes to write down their stories, so therefore, many true meanings of events were lost by not using the correct words and the scribes misunderstanding of the words spoken to them.

One great example of misunderstanding and wrong words usage is; people thinking of God as being a person-like Entity and Him standing as a Ruler or King who controlled and punished his subjects, and Jesus as Lord – one how is overseer of the land.

And whenever we think of God as a being that is human-like, we created a god who hates and loves the things that we do. And in which

Christianity, Hebrew and Islamic Religions are full of misconceptions about God, because they view Him as being a human-like Entity. As if, we are the center of the Universe, and were the most intelligent beings ever created.

One more item must be discussed before we finish the look at the Bible, and that is "Time."

Time is the symbolic measurement for length of life. The measurement of time that we use comes from the revolutions of our planet, Earth, which also includes our world revolving around the star, which we call our Sun. These are things of this dimension and they are not things of God's plane. But yet, God's plane and our dimension are running parallel to each other.

An Entity, which can be either good or bad, can enter and interact with us in our dimension at this time, but They cannot go back in time to re-enter. They may only go back in time to re-view events that occurred in this dimension as the Entity stands on his plane. For if they could re-enter the past, they could change events and that would change the future.

In the beginning there was the universe, but there was no matter, only a void and darkness, for the universe was the first thought of God in creating what we refer to as life. But then, He first created the void and darkness of the universe. Then, God created matter that slowly evolved – came together to form the things that surround us in the universe, including our world. Once God started His creation of His Master Plan, all was put into place as He allowed evolution, and it started to unfold. And from that point in which God created the universe, He knew the complete history of events to come as laid out in His Master Plan. Then, God implanted the feelings and all things that are needed by the individual types of life into the first one-celled living thing that lived. And what these feelings and things needed later come forth as needed by the different kinds of living things, including the things that separate humans from the animals; our ability to comprehend.

Saying that God created everything in six days and rested on the seventh is a concept of man, for time is irrelevant to God. And it does not matter if God could make everything in one minute, in one day or if it took millions of years to create. The seven day span of time mentioned only means a cycle of time that it took to form everything, and that cycle could have been any length of earthly time. For once He created the atomic matter and dust that is in the universe, His evolution, which is part of His Master Plan did the rest.

God and His Angels do not need rest. For rest is for the living because we extend ourselves and need to replenish our bodies, God and His Angels are Energy and do not need to be refueled.

The idea of God creating man in His image made people view God as if man looked and acted as God, thus causing men to see themselves as being equal to God. But God created man in His image as being able to think and to comprehend.

The story of Adam and Eve was conceived by man for better understanding of why we are here and to place man above woman. But the story does indicate that woman is equal to man and should stand beside man because she was made from his rib – something from his side, and someone to be loved as himself because she came from near his heart. And since God created woman last does that mean women are the finest of His Creations because she was His last Creation?

Wouldn't God have kept His best Creation for last?

Adam and Eve were innocent and as the Angels of God, Adam and Eve only had righteous thoughts and only ate the things that grew from the earth, except the fruit from the tree of Knowledge. The concept of eating of meat meant the killing of living things and killing is not in the thoughts of Angels.

The tree of Knowledge of right and wrong, was part of the Master Plan. Adam and Eve had to learn both, right and wrong to know self-judgment.

God knew what they would do, He knew that Eve would first taste the fruit from the tree. But God had told them to eat only the things that grew from the ground and not the animals, and not from the tree of life. God knew that Adam would listen to his wife, another human, and follow her in eating from the tree of Knowledge.

God did not condemn Eve and all women that proceeded her throughout time because He knew what she and Adam would do. Man condemned her - woman. Her act of eating from the tree was needed for humans to learn, grow and experience from their mistakes to correct their actions. Therefore, men should not have placed themselves above woman, for they – woman, are also part of the human race and equal to men.

The serpent was inserted into this story by man's ideas of snakes being evil, but God created serpents, too. And in some of the old religions, serpents are worshippded as gods. Do you think God would have created something that He did not like or knew was bad?

If you make something that you do not like such as something that is bad, you would destroy it, but God did not destroy the serpents. Therefore, nothing that is here is evil, bad or to be hated. Hatred grows from evil while love comes from God. There are levels of love, from the highest form of love – Divine Love down to dislike. Therefore, we should not hate anything, but we can dislike a thing or the actions of people. God created man, but people decide upon what to do, thus creating their own actions that may come from thoughts of good or evil.

The story of Adam and Eve in the Garden of Eden was created by man for man to follow concepts of others, and it was symbolic for people to follow their ruler or king, and this story was interwoven with God's words to keep people under domination from others, and yet, it does say many truthful things about God.

God is demanding but He does not dominate. Demanding is different than domination, example; you may demand that an electrician must be licensed before he makes repairs to the electrical wiring in your home. But you are dominating if you demand that the electrician must have studied only at ULCA before he can work on your home's electrical system.

Domination comes from trying to control others thus it comes from evil. God demands only that we are righteous in our actions and thinking before He will accept us as being part of Him as one of His Angels.

Throughout this story God is asking them questions, but He already knew their answers, for their answers were laid down (known) in His Master Plan.

Was He testing their honesty?

No!

He was allowing people to test themselves, to see what was right for them.

He knew their honesty because that was also known when He first Created the universe.

He was allowing them to experience the feelings of lying to Him. For experiencing the feelings and judging between right and wrong are the reasons for life. God has given all, including Adam and Eve, individual choices in life. If God dominated people, he would have not given Adam and Eve a chance to answer His questions because He knew what they had done.

After Adam and Eve tells God that they have eaten from the tree of Knowledge, Adam tells Eve, "You will bear children with intense pain and suffering. And through your desires will be for your husband, he will be your master."

It is written that it was God and not Adam that told Eve these things, and it does not say that God told of these things to all the women who would come after Eve. And God did not and does not punish women for what Eve did, but men are still punishing women for what Eve did. All female animals including woman go through pain and suffering when giving birth of offspring, and not just human women. Therefore, God did not place punishment on all female animals for what one woman did because pain and suffering are a natural part of giving birth to offspring. And the amount of divorces we have in the world today indicates that women were not damned to the desires of their husbands because women are not merely slaves as in Islam. In the last part of God's statement to Eve, did God or Adam say, "he (male) will be your master,"

Therefore, did God divide man and woman into different classes or did man?

Would a loving God place one class of people (women) in slavery and make another (men) as their master?

And if gender is reason for classification then, how about the color of skin?

God did not make one person better than another, for all life is grandeur to Him. A loving Father does not place any of His children in slavery, but instead, allows them to choose their own direction in life. Thus, God has given all of us our own individual choices in life.

Then, God said, "The people have become as we are, knowing everything, both good and evil."

To live as human, one must know the difference between good

and evil for one to judge one's individual actions. You cannot judge anything if you do not know its opposite. Did God want people not to be human?

No!

He wants all people to have personal and individual choices but to know the difference between good and evil so we will make the right decisions.

Then God said, "He who ate from the fruit of the tree of life can live forever!"

(Those who have the Knowledge of God, all humans, that will use the knowledge throughout their daily lives may live forever with God Forever. The life that people lived will be a continual part of God as their Soul.)

Was there a tree of life in the Garden?

That is a big mystery of the Old Testament, but the biggest mystery in Genesis is where did Cain's wife come from?

And who did Abel marry?

Most theologians will say that Cain's wife was his sister. But the story does not say that nor does it say anything about Adam and Eve having daughters. The Jewish religion claims that they were the chosen people of God's, and they were the only people created by God, and they do not believe in incest, then where did their daughter-in-laws come from?

All of these questions leave no doubt that man's ideas, concepts and thoughts were placed into the story of Adam and Eve, and this was the primary reasons for the writings in the Old Testament because man wanted control and domination over other people. And yet, most of the Old Testament can be used for living a good life, and should be read as historical fact and to realize that God and His Angels have inter-reacted with humans throughout and including our present time.

After Adam and Eve are kicked out of the Garden of Eden, they then have two sons, and the family survives by farming and raising live stock. Their oldest son, Cain was a farmer while Abel was a shepherd. At harvest time, Cain gives an offering of farm produce to God while Abel makes an offering of lambs from his flock. God approves of Abel and his offering, but does not approve of Cain or his offering.

(Keep in mind that while Adam and Eve lived in the Garden, they lived next to animals and only ate things that grew from the earth. And just before God expelled them from the Garden, He made clothing out of animal skins for them because He would not allow them to kill animals. He did not approve of humans killing animals, and He cared about Adam and Eve just as you would not want your children going outside without warm clothing. Therefore, He made sure they were dressed warmly before they left.)

Cain kills Abel after God has rejected him and his offering. And then, God questions Cain about Abel's murder and banishes Cain to the land of Nod.

But God did not allow humans to kill animals in the Garden, but he approved of killing of animals outside of Eden as indicated by His approval of Abel's offering. Thus, God's disapproval of Cain and his offering occurred because of what was in Cain's heart, and not from what Cain offered. For there is no need to offer anything other than yourself to Him.

Cain then tells God, "You have banished me from my land and from your presence; you have made me a wandering fugitive. All who see me will try to kill me."

Is Cain the first Arab – Muslim, and is this the first mention of the time to be known as Armageddon?

Is this the separation between the Jew and Muslim?

The book of Genesis does not say who were the ones who Abel thought would try to kill him, but it does indicate that only Adam, Eve and Cain were alive when this statement was made. Then, it talks of Cain's wife giving birth in the land of Nod. If you believe that the Holy Bible is the true words of God, then, you must accept the fact that Cain married some "thing" or someone outside of his immediate family who he may have met in Nod. For the Holy Bible does not say that he married his sister, but also, it does not say that Cain met or married his wife in the land of Nod. Later in Genesis it does talk about descendants of Cain being women, but up until the time that Cain left his land, there is no mention of women.

Our calendar is based on Christianity, and it has been in existence for a short period of time compared to the age of the world. Before its creation and during the time Old Testament stories were lived many calendars were in use. And most people did not even know their own age. For time of the day and day of the year are merely indications of what they have or have not accomplished during their lives. But, accomplishments are self-centered. God and His Angels do not have the knowledge of self-centered feats, but all is known in the Master plan.

(Presently, most parts of the world use the Gregorian calendar. It was conceived by Pope Gregory XIII during 1582 AD, to correct the Julian year to the astronomical year, the first being the Old Style (*O.S.*) date and the second being the New Style (*N.S.*). We cannot truly understand or know what kind of calendar was used during the days of Adam and Eve. But if we use a calendar based on the cycle of the Moon, at the age of 57 years old, it could be said that David is 684.)

The Book of Revelation written by St. John is very similar to what is written in the Book of Daniel. Therefore, St. John may have seen the same things that Daniel saw or he may have merely copied Daniel's visions into his words, and we will never know which, but we surely should understand that both men reported what they thought they had seen. For each account of what was to come, was viewed symbolically for them as individuals, and each man interpreted their visions into words that were used and understood during the days of their lives.

David has learned through his visions and conversations with God's Angels, that we do not always receive things in their correct order, and they will use words that we do not have and words that we cannot comprehend their meanings. Therefore, the orders of events as described in Revelations are not accurate, and the events are corrupted through the usage of our words. This occurs because in this three-dimensional plane that we live in, we see and think of things as material and solid matter while the Angels speak of things as feelings. For feelings are things impressed upon Energy. When Energy is expressed using a capital "E," the word "Energy" is referring to God.

When Angels speak of feelings, we may interpret Their words as geographical locations and things including people. But feeling have location in time and this is merely a part of the Angels communications that St. John and Daniel could not conceive.

We need to discuss one more item of God's Creation that referes to as Revelations before I continue telling you the rest of our true story. The story of Revelations relates to the Knowledge that God instilled into man.

In the Book of Revelations, St. John said near its end; "And if any man shall take away from the words of the book of this prophecy, God shall take away his part out of the book of life, and out of the Holy City, and from the things which are written in this book."

That is truly ignorant to think that one person alone communicated with God's Angels and that he alone understood exactly the meanings of words spoken by God's Angels. Of course God's Angels have communicated with humans many times throughout history and He will continue His communications long after David am gone. Therefore, David knows that those He communicates with in the future shall view things differently than he has written, but while their visions may have been the same.

And the Angel Jo said unto David, "The end is coming as truly as the sun came up today, but you should not look with despair, seek life - enjoy and experience the endurances that you have chosen for yourself. Love all others for what they are, human with part of God within, the part of God that is within them is the Angel-within. Do not allow others to place you in Hell. Do not take chances with your Soul or your body - keep them safe from harm, protect yourself. For all is yours that you wish.

"Desire that which brings you closer to God, wish for the good things in life. Do not lust for material things. Do not dominate your Angel-within, allow Him to seek God, then, you shall know God by the inspiration of Him that dwells within you. For your body is His vessel - His house that God created.

"The Book of Gabrael that is mentioned in Daniel is opened, but you nor anyone else shall reveal its complete contents. They and you may speak of things that indicate the end is near, but its date shall never be known until then. For if the end were known, people would live under its domination and not on faith and belief. Those are the 'gifts' from God that allow all humans their individual choices.

"Not even you, one who We have told, shall fully understand until you stand beside Me on this, the Other Side. For even you must live with the faith and belief in Us and in what We have said.

"It does not matter if your faith and belief comes from reading your Bible or direct communications, it is still your faith and belief in

God, for you have individual choices to decide your endurances in life.

"As you have read, 'One knows he has created his god when his god hates the same ones that he hates.'

"Many times you did not agree with the true God that We speak of, but with time you were inspired to realize that He was correct and you were wrong. Therefore, you did not create God, He created you, and therefore, He and I are real.

"We allow you to follow the things that you believe true, but whenever you go wrong, We stand fast with God, you need to do the same with others. Allow others to worship the gods that they have created, but do not allow them to drag you into their Hells, nor allow them to injure you or others. For if others desire to follow a man made god, allow them their choice, but cry for the dead, for those shall not know Heaven. And yet, inspire others to know God whenever they seek God through you.

"Teach those who wish to know, but do not place demands upon them.

"Do not twist our teachings of God into your concepts.

"Teach freely from your heart - the Angel-within and not from the dog.

"God has not placed demands on you or anyone else, do not place man-made demands as though from God upon those who desire to know the true God that Abraham, Isaac and Jacob worshipped, and Who is the same One that you worship. And yet, sometimes, you may as others, have placed their thoughts of others and others' actions over God's, and when this happens, remember Jesus or Me, and We along with the Angel-within you shall be there to help guide you, for We shall not demand you."

And then Jesus appeared and said unto David, "You cannot unravel a strand from part of life and understand it, for all is interwoven. And yet, you shall never understand life in the Master Plan until you stand outside of life that you know. As I told you previously, 'Speak to others as I have done. Tell them of the pains and hurts in your heart.' Do not speak of the past from the Bible, for God's Love will flow in your words. Those words will inspire others to seek God. This is what We have done with you, We allowed you to seek God in the time that you needed. For when you were ready for the job, the job was ready for you. Allow others their individual choices, too. You have repented from your past, you know others will repent as you did, if you approach them as We approached you with Inspiration."

And the Angels sang out in rejoice for David had completed God's teachings and was prepared for the job that was ready for him.

Life Continues

As David remembered back to the date when he, our youngest son and I were flying back to Ohio on July 19th, of 2001, for a long weekend and to visit with his oldest brother, Jim, who was very ill and dying from old age, Jim was 77, and David was 57. Even though there is a great difference in their ages, throughout David's younger years they did many things together. David remembered when he was pretty young, Jim had an Indian Motorcycle. He would pick David up and give him a ride on his motorcycle. It was just a small jaunt around the backyard, but David remembers thinking that it was the greatest thing in the world.

Jim would take the younger boys hunting and fishing, although they were always anxious and raring to go, Jim was always laid back and never in a hurry to do anything. One Saturday morning Jim told them that he would drive them out to the lake to go fishing. Well, he kept piddling around and David finally asked him if he was going to drive them to the lake or were they going to walk. David guessed in some ways Jim was like a second father to him, even though his father and him, along with his other siblings, did many things together.

But on Wednesday, the 18th of November, 2001, David, our son and I spent the night at a motel in Burbank, California. Early the next morning, we drove to the Burbank Airport and was waiting on our flight to Ohio. As we boarded the airplane, David told me that he had a bad feeling about this trip. Throughout the first leg of our flight, this bad feeling remained with him. At our first stop in Phoenix, Arizona, he could not contain this bad feeling any longer. We retrieved our luggage, rented a car and returned to California. Shortly after midnight on Friday, the 20th, David had another massive heart attack, his second heart attack, and after I called 911, he was rushed to the hospital.

By 4:30am, the ER staff was instructed to call in their CATH Team, who inplanted two more stents and used ballons to open two other blocked arteries and he was resting. Around 11:00am on Monday, David was released and went home to recover.

Later that evening, as he sat alone in a chair on the patio in our back yard garden, the Angel Jo appeared in front of him and extended her hand toward him. He somehow knew that She did not want him to stand but instead She desired that he remained sitting and to take Her hand in his, and this he did.

As David held Her hand in his, the Angel Jo said unto him, "We are individuals and yet, We are One."

As She spoke these words, Her appearence manifested from being that of the Angel Jo into the Angel Gabrael, and then into the Angel Michael and finally to Jesus, then Jesus, and He said unto him, "For We are God... for All in the universe is God."

David continued to hold the hand that was first the Angel Jo's and now was the hand of Jesus, as He continued and said unto David, "God does not make mistakes, humans do that for Him.

"We Inspired you to learn of God, this you did as others before you have done, and yet, those of the past have polluted God's Words with human thoughts, ideas and concepts, and this you shall not, while others of the past and present corrupt God's Words into domination of his fellow man. And yet, God allows this because We do not dominate for We only desire that you experience from the endurances of your life that you have chosen.

'Do not feel special for you are no better or no less than all others. For life may not seem grand but all life is grandeur to God, as even the life and experiences of the homeless are just as important as that of a king.

"Just as you and all other living are the same as I, who is the Master but also the Servant, for We are one with God, for We are part of God. But when not in congregation as God, we stand alone as individuals. Therefore, your human brothers and sisters are part of you as you are part of them, and yet, they too are individual but still part of God.

"Can you do anything but love yourself?

"Can you do anything but love God because He is part of you?

"His love remains because it is chisled in stone as your love of life is also chisled into the past.

"If you inflict pain or domination onto your left hand, does not the hurt injure the body?

"Does it not hurt the one who places another in sadness with God?

"And yet, the feelings of the dog are real but must be controlled. The feelings of the dog are for experiencing the endurances of human life for human life is that of the dog.

"God does not need human life, humans depend on God for life.

"When the Angel Jo told you about comforting the ill and to cry with the others, who was the ill that She spoke about?

"Who was the others She said to cry with?

"Are you not both - the ill and the sad?

"For We are all One.

"We stood beside you and guarded and protected you from the first onset of your heart attack and thoughout your stay in the hospitals as We do daily for you. We have kept our promise with you as you have kept your promise with Us.

"Now rest my brother, and enjoy and experience life to its fullest, for We shall continue to stand beside you and your family.

"All that happens was needed to happen."

And then He was gone.

And David cried as he prayed, "Father, thank You for all that You have given me, I will not fail You. Amen."

So many times in his life he has felt alone and confused and frustrated. As he sat there at his brother's funeral, reflecting back on all that he has learned from the Angels, he feels so truly blessed. There is a lot he had done in his past that he is not proud of, but he now has the knowledge of God's love and knows that, without a doubt, God is real and how much He loves him. He had repented from his past and prays everyday for God's guidance to help him be a better person.

As the funeral for James E. Haven finished, David watched as the people slowly went up to the casket to look at him one more time and say their last good-byes, as they called it, and David could not help but feel sad for them. If only they understood. Jim is no longer in the agonizing pain. His legs no longer hurt him, his organs do not have to work anymore. He no longer takes those trips to the hospital for dialysis. His body has departed from his soul. It will now return to the earth from which it came. His Angel with-in was now free to return Home. David could not help but wonder once again if the mourners' tears were because they were just missing him or because of how they treated him?

Did they wish they would have gone fishing with him one more time or maybe they should have spent that afternoon with him instead of watching the game on TV?

Did their brother, Espie, from Tennessee wish that he would have made that trip up to Ohio to see Jim a couple of weeks earlier?

David followed along in the procession as they drove into the cemetery where they laid Jim's body to rest along side of his loving wife. A thousand thoughts of cherished memories flashed through his mind, not only of his deceased brother and his family, but, also, of their remaining siblings and their families. How sad that they all seemed to have forgotten all of that.

After the funeral, everyone got together, as families do, to have a little celebration of Jim's life. David hugged all of his siblings and hugged everyone who allowed him to do so, and let all of them know that he loved them. David was talking with one brother and through the crowd of people he saw his brother, Dean, who was just a couple of years his senior. They just nodded and smiled at each other and when he finished his conversation and turned to look for Dean again, he was gone. David hadn't seen him in about fifteen years or so, and he knew fifteen years ago that he would never see him again.

David spoke of God's words of love and comfort to his siblings and his brother's children. He planted the seed. Only God knows what His Master Plan is from here.

Then after coming home from his brother's Funeral, Jesus was there again in our garden and said unto him, "Come to Me and I will hold you and comfort you, and We shall weep together.

"You just returned from driving across the United States to attend your eldest brother's funeral, and now, we stand in the garden once again. You went not to see Jim for the last time, you said your goodbyes last October when you visited with him, this time you traveled there to comfort and weep with those who mourned him. And yet, you mourned 7 days for the deceased and cry forever for the dead of the world as you were instructed, for you know the truth that the dead shall never know.

"Do you reall, when you were there, you talked with a man by the name of Rev. Jim Dye, who officiated over your brother's funeral. He stated that he feared that most of the people in the church were not saved. How correct he was, he is also lost for he believes that the only way to salvation is through Me. His throughts of salvation causes him to place domination over others. This is not the way to the Father, this is the way of the dead to death.

"When I first said, 'Come to me and I will hold you and comfort you, and We shall weep together', I was in human body, and all humans should say that to their sisters and brothers. The Christian Bible was written to demonstrate how you are to live and treat each other, for I am not the only one who can comfort you.

"One of your brother-in-laws said to you, 'I don't see why people cannot follow the Ten Commandments and the Golden Rules,' once again, the Christian Bible was written as a guide-line to live life by, but the people cannot understand what We meant. How sad to see humans destroy each other for their man-made gods, and yet, We have given them their individual choices in life.

"Your decisions are your individual choices and those you chose are Righteous as instructed by God. Blessed are those who follow God in faith and belief. You shall live in the House of Jacob - God's House - the Light forever."

And then the He was gone.

And David prayed, "Father, thank You for giving me the guidance of Jesus and Your Angels. My Lord, the True and Righteous Holy God above all, thank You for all that You have given us. Forgive me of my sins and help me understand them so that I will not commit them again. Guide and protect us as I continue and head for another day. Amen."

And then the Angel Jo appeared and said unto David, "My dearest David, you view death as We know about death, it is not the end to life but a change from death to life. You live in a world that is comprised of death, for all that is around you have came from dead things to live in the life that they know. But at the end of human life, one only removes the body and still lives but then, as part of God in the Heaven that one has made for himself. You cannot explain this to others because they must endure what they must learn as experiences.

"Do not feel bad because you know things that they do not understand, they could if they wished to know, but they do not wish it. One can only understand what one knows. We have inspired you to learn of true life with the Father, while they have learned about human life and have only taught you about life as human, you see and understand both. And yet, comfort them who do not understand God. The words of wisdom that you say can be said in ways that comfort those with either or both knowledge. And yet, try to inspire them to learn about God, but do not force your knowledge upon them. We only desire the best for all, and We will not force the Father upon them nor did We force Him upon you.

"Last fall, you saw your ill brother and said your goodbyes, then your wife and son wished to see and speak with him one last time, but that could not be. Cherish the good experiences you had with your brother for you know he only shed his body and will remain alive as part of God, living the Heaven that he has made for himself. But allow them to express and feel their feelings for those are the experiences that they must endure."

Life continues after death; the life that we have lived is there with God and His Angels on the Other Side. We do not continue to live as we did here on Earth, but the experiences of our lives will continue to be present and live forever with God, if that is what we desire.

Many readers might be asking the question, "So, where did David's brother go?"

The answer is, it is not David's concern. His concern is; He wishes his Angel to be able to re-live his life. And that decision about his life is left up to him. His brother may well be oblivious to God or his life experieces may dwell in God's Heaven. David's only concern is the things that he did to and against another, and those actions will live in his heart forever. David hopes his brother's Angel may go back and re-live their lives. If he allows it, but that, too, is not David's concern.

As David recalls, at the end of the Serivce for the Funeral for his brother, Jim, the room was silent as the mourners filed by to see his brother for the last time. And then he walked by him.

David stood there for a minute and prayed, "Dear Father, please comfort, protect and hold my brother, James Estil Haven, in Jesus' name, Amen."

If you grade life as "A" to "F", you should know that most of life isn't perfect, and anything lower than an "A" is an "F". And therefore, most everything that occurs in life must be an "F" because life is not perfect. We cannot expect life to always be an "A", we should try to raise the little part of our lives to be better.

Life is not a dress rehearsal, we will not be back again. Expect the best, but prepare for the worst because life is short. And once life is over, its over.

David recalls that me and some others think that he is cold and callous about death, but he understands what life and death is about, but he does not express sorrowful feelings when it comes to death.

Yes, the body goes through much pain at death, but that pain is no longer than a wink of the eye compaired to Eternity.

And David sings and rejoices with God's Angels at the deceased's Home coming as Grabael blows His horn, and he proclaims, "Wow, what a ride!"

www.ingramcontent.com/pod-product-compliance
Lightning Source LLC
Chambersburg PA
CBHW031604260626
47154CB00020B/1575